A Frost of Cares

Amy Rae Durreson

Published by Amy Rae Durreson, 2020.

For H, because we made it out alive. And for everyone else who has ever found themselves in a relationship collapsing because of depression or mental illness. There is light at the end of the tunnel. I promise.

They sought her that night, and they sought her next day,
And they sought her in vain while a week passed away;
In the highest, the lowest, the loneliest spot,
Young Lovell sought wildly—but found her not.
And years flew by, and their grief at last
Was told as a sorrowful tale long past
— From "The Mistletoe Bough," Thomas Haynes Bayly, 1830
My prime of youth is but a frost of cares
— From "Tichborne's Elegy," Chidiock Tichborne, 1586

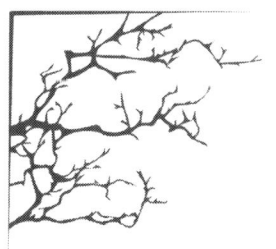

Chapter One

In a way this story begins with me standing by the window of my London flat on Boxing Day with a cricket bat in my hands, seriously considering smashing every bloody fucking pane of glass in the bloody fucking flat into bloody fucking shards. The thing that stopped me, in the end, was the handle of the bloody bat, wrapped in a fraying green grip. The end of the grip was peeling up, and that tiny imperfection, that little spike of lighter green, by being out of place, threatened to tear open the whole grip. Staring at it, I realized that I didn't know whether the bat was mine or Danny's.

Well, fuck, I thought. You'll have to excuse the paucity of my vocabulary at this point in the story. Obviously I was drunk as the proverbial skunk, and several of its cousins as well, and I never was much good at talking about my (bloody fucking) feelings.

The bat could have been mine. For two brief summers as a gangling teenager, I had been a proud but somewhat unlikely member of my school's second eleven. It hadn't lasted, and I couldn't remember if I'd kept any of that once treasured kit or whether it was in Mum and Dad's loft with the other detritus of our childhoods.

Danny, on the other hand, was keen on every sport going: cricket, rugby, tennis, golf, football, anything that can be discussed in arcane and passionate depth with complete strangers —or as he used to put it, *I like anything with a nice set of balls*. And there was the dilemma. If this was Danny's bat and I damaged it by using it on the windows.... It was unthinkable. What if he came home and found out I'd wrecked his stuff and so turned back round and walked away again?

Of course, by then I was 90% convinced that Danny was never coming home. He'd been missing for almost a decade, after all.

And that was why I didn't break any windows. Instead I put the bat down, poured myself another drink, and decided to get the fuck out of London.

And by "another drink," I mean the rest of the bloody pack, obviously.

Okay, maybe that wasn't the best place to start this story, because I'm pretty sure right now you're just thinking about what a sad and lonely fuckup this loser narrator is. Was. I've changed. Honest. Of course, I've no idea who "you" are. Who the fuck am I even writing this down for? I know what happened. I remember every moment of it. The only reason I'm trying to write this is because Jay thinks I'm clinging onto it a little too hard.

"Ten years ago, now," he said to me yesterday, calmly challenging in that way only Jay can be. "You're okay. Maybe, y'know, let it go? Let her go."

"She *is* gone," I reminded him. Of that, at least, I'm sure.

"Not if she's still in your head." He propped his chin up on his fist and looked at me, calm, steady, and analytical. (I still think of it as his "army face," though I never knew him while he was still on active duty.)

"I hardly ever think about it."

He smiled at me, wry and knowing. "Yeah? How many times this month have you slept with the light on?"

"Fuck off. Hardly any."

"Twelve. I know because I'm in the bed with you."

Hard to argue with that. "I can't just switch bad dreams off."

"You're not going to be that guy."

"What guy?"

"Never gets over seeing a ghost. Sits there in the old people's home trying to scare all the nurses. I'm not letting you."

"What am I supposed to do about it, then?"

"Get it out of your system," he said and shrugged. "Write it down. Lock it away somewhere and stop thinking about her."

I'm not convinced it's going to work, but Jay asked, and since he did, I suppose I have to try. He doesn't ask me for much. So I suppose I'm my own audience, or perhaps I'll do the traditional thing and one day pass on a flaking and dusty, well, Word document to some eager young great-nephew.

Or not.

Jay has just leaned over my shoulder and asked why I'm writing about hypothetical nephews. Fair question, though he blatantly knows the answer as well as I do.

I do like the smell of procrastination in the morning.

Also coffee. I like coffee. Perhaps I need to make some to help me get started. Mmm, coffee. Or tea. A whole pot, brewed from the leaf, slowly strained and served with Rich Tea biscuits. I don't think we have any Rich Teas. I could just pop out to—

Okay, and that was the point where Jay took my tablet away and made disappointed faces at me. No more procrastinating. I'll be good.

I don't want to write about her. What if it brings her back?

My husband is now trying to bribe me with filthy promises. Cheater.

Okay.

Here goes, in proper ghost story style:

The professor first went down to E—— Hall on the 27th December 20—. At the time when he boarded the train at Waterloo, he had little apprehension that—

No, can't do it. Bit too much of the M. R. James in that, and I never liked old Monty much. Too much prose, too little action, and far too many phobias of damp and hairy things lurking under the bed, poor closeted git.

Truth is, I wasn't in a fit state to be apprehending anything that day, because I was as hungover as one of those aforementioned skunks would have been if they tried to sleep it off in the bottom of a hop kiln. It was late afternoon by the time I got to the station, and I had to wait ages for a train. I'd managed to stumble over to my estate-agent sister's that morning, timing it for while Mum and Dad were out taking their Day After Boxing Day stroll across the common, and I'd tossed my key at Katie before I could change my mind. I'd told her to go ahead and do what she'd been begging me to do for years: shove my crap and Danny's into storage and put the flat on the market.

I'd finally had enough of waiting.

I was regretting it bitterly by the time I got to Waterloo, but I resisted the urge to phone Katie and tell her I'd changed my mind. Enough was enough.

If Danny came back while Katie was there, she'd make sure he stayed around long enough for me to rush back up to town. I trusted her, even though it galled me to ask my little sister to clean up the mess that was my life.

I had enough self-awareness to know I couldn't do it without help, though.

I actually had a good reason to be leaving London. "Professor" is a bit of a stretch, but I was already steadily on the academic career path. I was a Junior Research Fellow at one of the lesser-known London colleges, specializing in the nineteenth-century development of the British Army. I'd done a lot of work with military archives before, and my PhD supervisor, now my boss, had done considerably more.

At the time I went to Eelmoor Hall, the Army was in a state of quiet upheaval. After seventy years, it had just been announced that they would be withdrawing British troops from Germany. By the end of 2016, the Army claimed at the time, 11,000 troops and 17,000 support staff and family members stationed overseas would be back in the UK. To house them, there needed to be a vast reorganization of British Army bases. Barracks that had long stood empty were being spruced up, and regiments and organizations were being relocated all over the country.

One of the many changes underway was the relocation of the Royal Military School of Medicine from its traditional home in North Hampshire to a cheaper and more modern campus in the northeast. The RMSM had been housed in Eelmoor Hall, between the towns of Fleet and Aldershot, since 1923, and as part of the move, their CO had written to my supervisor to ask if he could recommend a keen young chap who might be interested in spending a few weeks cataloguing and organizing their archives and small museum in preparation for the move. They were offering a decent wage, it would get me out of London for a few weeks, and they were putting me up for free in the now empty hall itself.

Jay says I'm waffling again, bloody backseat driver that he is.

Well, that got rid of him, though I'll have to offer makeup sex later. So, where was I?

Eelmoor Hall.

It was dusk by the time the taxi drew up at the gates, the sort of dull winter dusk that is only the steady fading of a grey day into true darkness. There was supposed to be an on-site caretaker, one Sergeant McBride, who would let me in the gate. I climbed out of the taxi to hit the buzzer on the intercom and started to shiver. The air here was noticeably crisper than it had been in London, and my breath immediately rose in clouds.

Sergeant McBride took his time answering and was curt when he told me to wait until the gate opened. I shoved my hands into my pockets and took another breath of that cold air. It tasted cleaner than London air, and I squinted through the gates to see the grounds of Eelmoor Hall. There were lawns on this side, and a long drive running towards a pillared frontage. The old house had two wings that stretched back from the main front so the hall was longer than it was wide, and I knew there were a number of modern buildings in the grounds behind it—offices, accommodation and teaching rooms—as well as several assault courses and firing ranges. The archive was in the library, in the east wing of the old hall.

Standing there, gazing up at the stark lines of the hall, it looked as dark and tired as I felt, its redbrick frontage turned brown by the fading light. The windows were dark, but I could easily imagine that someone was standing in there, hidden behind the heavy curtains and watching my approach.

The gate whirred open, and I scrambled back into the taxi. When we finally drew up on the front drive, a man was waiting by the front entrance, leaning back against the base of the right oriel window with his arms crossed. He wore a khaki jacket and had a woollen cap pulled down low, although a few fair curls escaped around the back. He didn't say anything as I paid the driver and lugged my case up the low steps. Only when I put it down at the top did he nod to me. "Dr Alcott, I presume?"

"Luke," I corrected him and held out my hand. "You must be Sergeant Mc—"

"Jay. Not in the Army much longer." His voice was flat. "Was expecting you a little earlier."

That explained his bad mood. In the emotional tumult, I'd forgotten to phone and let him know I was running several hours late. "Shit, I'm so sorry. It's been a day, man. I didn't mean to—"

"Library key," he cut over me, handing an old brass key over. "Master key for bedrooms and kitchens, passcode for the gate and external doors, which changes on Saturday. You're in Room 221. The corridor can be accessed from the main stairs or the library gallery. Crates and packing material are in the ground floor store cupboard by the main library door. If you get lost or need something, I'm on extension 445, unless I'm at work."

"And then?"

"I'm at work. This isn't my main job."

"Then I'm even more sorry to have screwed with your day. Don't the Army pay a proper wage for this?"

He lifted one shoulder in a slow shrug. "They just don't want the place to sit here empty. I live here and keep an eye on things, and they don't charge me rent."

"Oh, the property-guardian thing. Couple of my grad students do that. Always thought it sounded like a bit of a scam, but this looks like a nice setup." I was babbling, thrown by his grim, unresponsive face. He was handsome, now I looked properly, and that just made me want to talk more. "I mean, it must be good to have a whole bloody mansion to call your own. Or the Army's own, I suppose, though—" I made a conscious effort to stem the word-dribble. "Um. So. I should be getting inside."

He didn't move, but a faint hint of amusement around his eyes salted the grimness. He had an accent, faintly underlaying everything he said with that peculiarly Ulster combination of musicality and muscle. "If you like."

He clearly wasn't going to come with me, and I bit back a little irritation of my own. Okay, so I'd inconvenienced him, but he didn't have to be rude. "Point me in the right direction?"

"East," he said and pointed. "Thataway."

"Cheers," I said and lugged my case inside. I glanced back to see him still leaning against the wall, scowling out over the now shadowy line of the drive where it curled back towards the gates and the lodge.

Look, I never claimed it was love at first sight.

Inside, the foyer had that odd mixture of institutional function and faded grandeur that seems to characterize old schools and posh hotels. It was dark, but lights came on as I moved forward, triggered by some motion sensor somewhere, and I was able to follow signs to the library, the lights rising and fading as I walked. I stopped for a moment at the bottom of a stairway, wondering whether it was a shortcut to my room or whether I should just carry straight on and find the way through the library.

I must have stood still too long for the motion sensors, because the lights went off. It was dark—country dark, not London dark—with no lights outside to shine through the windows, and suddenly the big house seemed even vaster and colder. I could hear a faint rattling in the wall, a distant electronic hum from somewhere, a creak of floorboards upstairs, all the normal sounds of an old and empty building.

And, as you sometimes do in old buildings, I suddenly felt that I wasn't alone. I thought that someone else was there in the darkness, breathing in perfect time with me, so close that I could have reached out and touched them. I startled, and the lights came back on.

I was alone, of course, in an empty hallway filled with blank notice boards. It had just been my imagination.

I made my way to the library, and once I was there, I forgot all about the creepy hallway and Sergeant Arsehole McBride and got caught up in the work. They had records in there going back to the founding of the school, and the last catalogue had been done back in the eighties, when they'd actually employed a part-time archivist and librarian. His neat little cabinet of index cards was still there, although one glance showed me they were hopelessly muddled. Some of the newer material had been added, but that effort seemed to fizzle out in the mid-nineties. There was a computer, a PC old enough that it still had a floppy disk drive and a dial-up modem. A faded Post-it note on the front told me that it was available for half-hourly slots only ("Please do not abuse your extranet privileges").

So the first step would be to find out exactly what I had in here.

I'll spare you the details. I find them fascinating, but in the end they're not what this story is all about. What I do need to explain is what I was thinking about that first night in the library. Jay reckons, and I agree, albeit reluctantly, that if I had been any other type of miserable, I probably wouldn't have caught her attention in the way I did.

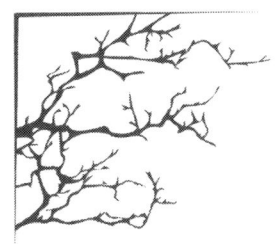

Chapter Two

I was thinking about Danny. By now, you've probably worked out that this wasn't unusual. Danny's absence had been the defining fact of my life for far longer than we'd ever been together. I was sick of it, but I couldn't just pretend it didn't exist. Despite my determination to move on, to finally put him behind me, I slipped too easily back into the usual kind of daydream—the ones where Danny came back, swept me up in his arms with a bright roar of laughter, or dropped to his knees before me, his eyes bright and his hand on his heart.

Stupid dreams, all of them. Danny and I had been on a bad road to nowhere before he left, and I had a crooked nose and a scar across my brow to prove it. I had loved him, though, even when our life went spinning out of control, and suddenly deciding that I didn't want him back felt like the last and worst betrayal.

I wanted my life back too, that was the problem. I wanted not to be alone. I'd had wildly romantic dreams once, about some perfect guy who would sweep me off my feet and worship me with his body, preferably in some warm and glamorous location where neither of us needed to wear very much or work for a living. These days, not being seventeen anymore, I'd adapted my expectations to reality a little. I wanted someone to be there with me when I woke up in the morning. I wanted someone who would comfort me and accept my comfort in return, someone I could rely on. Even if he did come back, Danny could never be that for me. I'd never be able to trust him that much, and I despised myself a little for that as much as I hungered for a kind touch.

So there I was in the library, doing an initial survey and feeling guilty about finally deciding to turn my back on our flat, when my phone rang. It was Danny's brother, Mark.

"Dude," he said when I picked up. "About bloody time."

"For what?" I asked warily.

"For you to get a fucking life of your own."

"Please tell me your kids aren't in the room."

"Nah, Ciara's taken them to the sales to spend their Christmas vouchers."

"How'd you land her with that one?" I asked. Mark's wife was dazzlingly sharp and brilliant, and no more keen on unbridled commercialism than I was.

"Tossed a coin. Now stop changing the subject, mate. What happened?"

"How'd you know?" I asked, wedging the phone under my chin as I tried to shift a slithering pile of files to the central table.

"Mum phoned." His voice sobered. "She's in a bit of a state."

"I'm sorry," I said, my heart sinking. My relationship with Danny's parents was a complicated mess. They believed, and I sometimes secretly agreed, that his disappearance was their fault.

Danny hadn't come out to them until after we had graduated in 2004 and started renting the London flat I now owned. It had been disastrous, on a no-son-of-mine scale I thought only happened in the Bible Belt, not the home counties. Overnight, Danny went from being their prized eldest son, the ex-cricket captain and head boy who had gone on to read law at Oxford, to being an outcast from his family.

When he disappeared, their attitude had changed, but by then it was too late. All their remorse never brought him home again. They had done a lot for me, though, pouring time and money into the search for Danny, dragging me into every family event with relentless determination to make good, lending me the money to put a deposit down to buy the flat in case he came back.

I'd long since paid them back, but I'd still felt duty bound to tell them about my decision, even before I called my own parents.

"Don't be sorry," Mark said sharply. "You should have done it years ago."

I let that pass. Mark had been a cocky sixteen-year-old the first time I met him, when he'd come up to visit Danny in our first year at Oxford, but even then he had idolized his big brother. He'd taken Danny's disappearance hard, angry where I was lonely. He'd been through dark years of his own, before Ciara got pregnant, but now he was my friend. Strange to think that I'd actually known him four times longer than I'd known his brother.

"Can't blame them for being upset," I said, wandering through the library. I liked to pace when I talked, and there was space for it in here. The main floor of the library was arranged on either side of a central aisle, with shallow shelf-lined bays opening out of it on either side. There was a bow window, with low shelves below it, and a small gallery above. I could spy a door that opened from it, and went in search of a way up as Mark snorted in my ear.

"What finally made you see sense?" he asked as I spotted the bottom of a narrow set of wooden steps.

I hesitated a little. It hadn't been a quick decision so much as a slowly building sense of exhaustion. Since April, I had slowly come to realize that I had no more energy for waiting. I gave Mark a simple answer, though. "Ten years since we had our first Christmas in the flat."

"Damn," he said softly, and then more forcefully, "My brother's an arsehole."

The stairs were a beautifully crafted wooden spiral, and I went up them with a sense of adventure. "No, he's not."

"He beat the shit out of you and ran away."

"You know that's not the whole story," I reminded him. "He was ill." The gallery at the top was just big enough for a long table and a few chairs, but the floors were scuffed and the whole area looked more used than the rest of the library. There were more low shelves along the balustrade, piled up with magazines.

I heard a soft creak from the other side of the door but dismissed it as I went to investigate. The first shelf was full of comics, much read. The next one explained why this part of the library was so well used and made me let out a whoop of laughter.

"What?" Mark asked. Outside the door, I heard another creak, a little farther away.

"I just found the squaddies' stash of girlie magazines."

He was silent for a moment. "Where *are* you?"

"Not far from you, actually. Eelmoor Hall. Research project."

"Never heard of it."

"Just outside Aldershot." There was another creak, and I suddenly put the sounds together. Someone was pacing up and down the corridor on the other side of the door. Grinning, I told Mark, "And squaddies is a bit unfair, since the lads here were all proper medics. Of course, now only Sergeant McDickhead is left to watch over, dear God, more copies of *Nuts* than I've ever seen in one place. No wonder he's pacing around outside. Probably worried I'm going to flog them to collectors on eBay."

"Sergeant Mcwhat? Have you already pissed off the natives?"

"The caretaker. Bit of an arse."

"Let me guess," Mark said. "Bald, homophobic, face like the back end of a bulldog?"

"Christ, what squaddies have you been hanging out with? Youngish—well, our age, could be hot if he wasn't a rude git."

"Oh, really?" Mark asked, sniggering.

"Oh, fuck off," I said back sweetly.

"I love you too, Sparklypants," Mark said and then added gleefully, "Oh, hi, Ciara."

"Nice try," I heard Ciara say in the background. "Wasted effort, though. I'm already leaving you after that morning of hell." I could hear the sound of squealing kids behind her, but she snatched the phone away from Mark. "Hey, Luke."

"I take it I'm the only Sparklypants in your husband's life," I said.

"The only one too old to own glittery My Little Pony knickers, yup."

"I'm too old for those? Damn. Someone should have told me. How were the sales?"

"Seventh circle of hell," she said flatly, and chuckled. "And now I know what we'll be getting you next Christmas. The girls would love it."

"Save them for Mark's birthday," I advised her, not without a sigh of relief. "Still on the Christmas card list, then?"

"Always," she said and added thoughtfully, "Who else am I going to get to babysit for free?"

"So kind." The sounds of small-girl excitement were getting louder behind her, so I added quickly, "Seriously, if you need a break, bring them over here. I've got the run of the place until the end of January, and the grounds are big enough to wear out even your hellspawn."

"You think you're joking," she muttered darkly. "Damn it, Mark, not the *Frozen* DVD *again*!"

"Go," I said, laughing. "Give the girls my love."

I was still smiling as I shoved my phone back into my pocket, and the rush of good humour sparked a bit of mischief in me. Flinging open the library door, I proclaimed, "Caught you!"

There was no one there. The corridor was dark, stretching out before me with only dim patches of moonlight falling through the windows to measure its length. There was no sound but my own breathing. Then a light hummed on above me and I thought I heard footsteps again, skittering away along the corridor.

Well, at least I'd successfully taken some mice by surprise. Feeling slightly abashed, I retreated back into the library and set to work again.

The next interruption was the growling of my stomach. I'd lost track of time completely and was slightly startled to find it was well past eight. Leaving the library, I went in search of my room. I didn't have far to go—room 221 was right outside that upper door. It had an en suite shower room and access to a poky little kitchen that had obviously been shared between half the corridor once. The kitchen was on automated lights as well, but the room, thankfully, was not. It felt like stepping back in time to my student days, complete with mini oven, folding table, and row of toasters.

Unlike a student kitchen, the place was spotlessly clean and completely devoid of anything even theoretically edible.

I still had some signal, just enough for my phone to tell me that I was outside the delivery area for all the Aldershot takeaways and that the nearest shop still open was a mile along a dark road. Bloody countryside.

I briefly considered calling a taxi to take me into town, but I was tired enough that it seemed too much hassle. I still had half a bottle of Coke and a packet of crisps I hadn't eaten on the train, so I made do and then crashed into the neatly made bed with a groan of relief. It had been quite a day, and I was drained enough that I fell asleep within moments, barely managing to switch the bedside lamp off before I was asleep.

MY SLEEP MIGHT HAVE been deep, but it was full of strange, fragmented dreams: firelight and fiddles playing, the heavy scent of evergreens, the echo of laughter. I dreamed that Danny came back, not to apologize, but to knock me down again and stand over me with his hands torn and bloody. Then he was gone and I was in the library of Eelmoor Hall, pacing between high shelves that never ended but simply opened into more aisles of dusty books and files, trapped in a maze of words.

I woke twice, and each time the darkness startled me into stillness. I had been in London for a decade, and before that there had been Oxford and the suburban Brighton of my childhood, places where streetlights shone past even the thickest curtains. Here there were no lights, and the darkness settled on me more heavily than the thin duvet.

The last time I woke, I couldn't move and I was afraid.

Put like that, the latter seems the obvious consequence of the former. In fact, they were quite separate sensations to begin with. It was the paralysis that I noticed first, when I tried to reach out for the lamp and my body simply refused to answer. I tried again and again, but I couldn't move. My body was pressed down against the sheets, a heavy cage of flesh. No matter how hard I tried to shift it, it didn't respond. I shouted, or tried to, but only a high whine made it out of my lips. I could feel every thread of the sheets and duvet pressing against me like strands of steel, but I couldn't move them, couldn't shape my mouth to turn my whine into words, couldn't roll or kick or slam my elbow against the wall.

At the same time, as I struggled against rising panic, something else was stirring in the room. It felt like static electricity, moving over my body in invisible, almost imperceptible ripples that made every hair on my body stand on end and the roof of my mouth prickle.

It wasn't electricity, though. It was fear.

I'm aware that sounds absurdly melodramatic. I can tell you, though, that of all the dark moments of my life, the ones I am most afraid of reliving are those moments there in the darkness of Eelmoor Hall with the fear washing over me.

It came in waves, each one starting with that low sense of unease and then building slowly, cold gathering at the back of my neck and the base of my spine. As it built, my stomach clenched, my heart quickened, and my breathing came faster. By the time it peaked, I was trying to scream. Then it faded, seeping away until my pulse slowed and I became aware that I was still frozen. Each time, I had just long enough to hope it was over and turn my attention back to trying to get some part of my body moving. Then that slow ripple of dread would stir the air, and it would all begin again.

I don't know how long it went on for. It felt like hours, but it could have been minutes. After a while, I stopped fighting and let it roll over me. I was shivering by then, the air so cold it stung my cheeks. At that moment, I knew with clear and absolute certainty that I was going to die right there, alone in the dark.

Eventually the fear stopped, although I still couldn't move. By then I was so drained that I didn't even try. Instead I simply lay there, staring up at where the ceiling must be.

There was a faint creak above me, and then another, the distinctive sound of someone pacing across the room above mine, their steps light and quick. Listening to those steps, I sank back into a state that was closer to stupor than sleep.

I woke some time later when my foot suddenly cramped and I kicked out in response, slamming it against the wall. With the action came the realization that I could move again, and I threw myself out of bed so fast I was light-headed before I even got to the window.

Outside, there was only the thinnest line of dawn along the horizon, but it was enough to make out the silhouettes of the trees that bordered the gardens and the dull gleam of the lake. I wasn't quite mad enough to open the window, not when I could already see the frost gleaming on the lawns, but I took several deep breaths of relief.

I couldn't sleep after that, so I had a quick shower and removed myself to the library. The physical work helped chase the last echoes of the bad night away, and I had soon logged one of the ground floor bays of books and files. Before long, the intensity of the fear had faded and I was feeling a little ashamed of myself. I'd had bad dreams after Danny left, but none that had ever left me quite so shaken. I'd thought I was made of stronger stuff, and as the day brightened into morning, I convinced myself that it had all been nothing, a mixture of low blood sugar, a long day, and the last remnant of a hangover.

That didn't stop me from leaping about a foot when someone knocked on the library door.

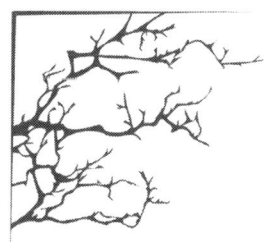

Chapter Three

"Getting started early?" Sergeant McBride inquired. He was leaning in the open doorway on the ground floor, his fist still raised from where he had tapped it against the door. At my no-doubt wild-eyed stare, he added, "Saw the lights on."

"Oh, right, yeah. Well, I was awake, so I thought I might as well. You know what it's like, first night in a strange place. Er." I stammered to a halt before it even occurred to me that I didn't owe this man an explanation. In fact, it ought to go the other way. He'd been the one pacing around upstairs at an ungodly hour of the morning, after all. I couldn't quite bring myself to challenge him, though. There was something quite unassailable about that stern face of his. I didn't get the impression that he was a happy man, but he was definitely one who belonged quite solidly within his own skin.

"You don't have wheels."

I actually looked down at my feet before I caught up with what he meant. "Oh, no. I work inside the congestion zone. Not worth it to keep my own car, and I can usually make do with buses, right? There's one here, isn't there?"

"Supposedly." His lip curled a little on the word. "I don't have to work until this afternoon."

"Okay."

He shrugged a little. "Thought this morning, when I saw your light, that you probably didn't have food in."

What was this, Non Sequitur World? "You'd be right, unfortunately."

"So." He nodded.

"So?"

He looked a little irritated. "*So*, do you want a lift to Morrisons?"

Oh. Obviously conversing with this man was going to take advanced deductive skills, but I wasn't going to turn the offer down. "If it's not going to put you out of your way."

"Need to go into town anyway. Be out the front in five."

"Mate, you're my new hero. Just let me grab my coat and wallet, and I'll be right there."

I was halfway up the stairs to the gallery before I realized how still he had gone. Then he said, every word slow and careful, "Don't call me a hero."

"Sorry," I said, a little rankled, and turned to frown at him. I'd been trying to be nice.

He was already leaving, his back to me. As soon as I saw him move, I realized why he was no longer on active duty, why he hadn't come in with me last night, and why it couldn't have been him I had heard pacing lightly above me in the night. His gait was slightly uneven, and each careful step he took with his left leg was accompanied by a faint mechanical whirr and a heavier thud against the floor.

He glanced back and caught me staring. Immediately, his lips narrowed and he said, tone too soft not to be dangerous, "See something interesting?"

"No. Um, yes? Er. Shit."

"If you're not in the car in five, I'm leaving."

"Right, of course, yeah. I'm moving. Okay." And I fled.

When I came out of the hall into a bright, crisp morning, the first thing I heard was the engine. The car looked like a fairly ordinary 4x4, but it emitted a low menacing growl that suggested somebody had done something very interesting to its innards. I climbed in the passenger side with a little trepidation, suddenly wondering exactly what McBride had done in the Army.

"You've got an hour, once we're in," he said. "Or you can get the bus back."

"An hour's plenty," I said and cleared my throat a little awkwardly. "Look, tell me to fuck off if it's an off-limits subject, but I'm sorry about your leg."

"Did you plant the IED?"

"No! How would I—"

"Then don't apologize." He started off down the drive faster than I would have done.

"'Fuck off' would have done quite nicely," I snapped at him, suppressing the urge to grab onto the sides of my seat.

He slowed as we approached the gates, and shot me a look. I couldn't tell if it was meant to be quizzical or threatening, but his tone was less defensive as he said, "Not off-limits, but watch your ste—be careful."

"Watch my *what*? Oh, God." I laughed before I could stop myself and then clapped my hand over my mouth. "Sorry. Shit."

The gates slid open, and he sighed with a note of frustration. "No worries. I'd have laughed too."

"I'm still sorry. Some things are due more respect."

"Laugh. I would if I could."

"When you can, let me know, and then it'll be okay for me to join in."

He grunted at me and accelerated down the lane. It was a narrow road with heathland spreading out on either side, yellow and damp in this season. In the distance, trees rose like brown bones along the side of the canal. The brightest thing out there was the sky, which was a keen, cold blue I never saw in town. It was beautiful, in a bleak way.

All too soon, that beauty yielded to the outskirts of Aldershot. It's an undeniably ugly town, a patchwork of pound shops and off-licenses, cheap shoe shops and dodgy takeaways, crammed into the battered shells of grand old Victorian buildings. McBride drew into a new underground car park, one that hadn't been there last time I came to Aldershot. He sat back in his seat and snapped, "Meet me back here at ten."

He didn't move himself, so I was left to get out and find the exit alone. At the foot of the escalator, I glanced back and saw him still sitting in the car, his hands hooked over the wheel and his expression bleak. I thought about going back, but by now I had an idea how well that would go down, so I continued up to a gleaming new supermarket surrounded by a parade of empty chain restaurants and a glass-walled budget hotel. This was new, and it felt clumsily glued onto the edge of town. I couldn't quite face the vast anonymity of the big supermarket, but I knew from previous visits that Aldershot was more diverse than this. I found a self-proclaimed International Superstore—all of four aisles, but every one of them crammed full of cheap Polish biscuits, bulk packs of rice and lentils, and crates full of fresh herbs, chilies, and watermelon—and stocked up on cheap food before wandering back through town. It's a funny place, Aldershot, grotty but so up-front about it that locals develop an odd sense of pride in its complete lack of charm (even its most loyal residents refer to it fondly as "All-the-shit"). A retired general had once told me with a guffaw that people who lived in Aldershot were there to clean the houses of those who lived in Guildford and Farnham, the more affluent local towns, which made me like

Aldershot more and him less, and I wondered how the recession had hit an already struggling place. It felt even more like a ghost town than it had five years ago, more shops boarded up or standing empty.

I beat McBride back to the car, but only by a few moments. He gave me a nod that was half approval and half annoyance and swung up into the driver's seat again. This time, watching, I saw the bar behind the seat that he was using for extra leverage. As I got in, he leaned down and did something that made his artificial leg let out a long beep.

"Needs to be turned off when I'm driving," he said.

"Okay." I wanted to know why, but his expression warned me off. I hadn't noticed him turn it back on when we arrived, and I wondered if he had waited until I was out of sight.

We drove back through the military town without talking. It was beginning to make me uncomfortable; I didn't even like being alone with my own silence. Being on the receiving end of someone else's again gave me the jitters, so I started talking. "So, what is the day job, then? Not something with regular hours, obviously."

"Nope."

"Can't see you doing retail, and you don't quite measure high enough on the chirpy scale for a call centre."

"How is this any of your business?"

"Researcher here. I do get paid for asking questions, which is a bonus for me, because I was born nosy."

"I've noticed."

"So, bar work?"

"Nope."

How good was the leg? Surely not something that kept him on the move. "Professional babysitter? Dog groomer?"

"No."

"Assassin?"

He was quiet for a moment, but then said, without the faintest change of tone, "I could tell you, but then I'd have to kill you."

"Not like you're short of places to hide a body," I agreed. "What do I have to do to stop you from hiding my lifeless corpse in a box in the basement? Cash? Sexual favours? Booze? Curry? I make a damn good curry, by the way."

"Guess you get to live, then." After a moment, he added, "Mechanic."

"What?"

"I'm a mechanic. Roadside assistance."

"Sure you are," I said breezily and tapped my nose. "It's okay, dude, I won't break your cover."

He let out a rough snorting sound. It took me a moment to recognize that it was a laugh.

Success went to my head. "I meant it about the curry, you know. That bloody place is giving me the creeps. I'll happily cook if it gets me some company for an hour."

"Sure." He was quiet for a moment and then said, "Something you should know before you ask me to dinner."

"Veggie? That's okay. I'm versatile."

"No." We turned back onto the road over the heath, and he said, very flatly, "I'm queer."

"What?"

"I like cock," he clarified.

"Well, so do I, but I wouldn't phrase it quite like that."

"Oh." He went quiet again, and I glanced across to see a faint blush rising on his cheeks. "Yeah. Right. Not had much practice at that."

"No worries. It didn't show *at all*."

"Cheers." I was beginning to recognize that extra flatness was meant as sarcasm, and it cheered me up. Maybe he wasn't so unreadable. Then he added, very cautiously, "So, er, curry?"

"Just curry!" I replied hurriedly. "Not anything else. Not that it's anything personal, y'know, just curry. As curry."

"Okay, then."

We drove on in awkward silence.

Back in the library, I got a lot done that day, most of it too tedious to relate, but I felt virtuous. I even went out for a quick walk just after lunch, exploring the formal gardens, all stark lines and dark earth in this season. It was a magnificent place, and I took quite a few pictures to stick up on Facebook.

That afternoon, my mum commented on every one of my Facebook pictures. Mark spammed me with pictures of My Little Pony-themed underwear. Katie e-mailed to ask me if I'd considered renting rather than selling, with a long breakdown of the financial advantages. I replied to them all and enjoyed the quiet of the library. It was a good kind of quiet, the kind of loneliness that doesn't come with city bustle outside constantly reminding you that the rest of the world is passing you by.

Then Danny's mum phoned.

"Luke?" she said when I picked up, and her voice was so thin and shaking that I knew this wasn't going to go well. "It's Yvonne."

"Hi," I said, sitting down in the window seat.

"I was wondering—well, your move... it wasn't because you remembered something, was it? Something about Danny, I mean, about why he might not be coming back."

I said no as gently as I could. How do you tell a mother that you don't want to love her son anymore? That the thought of him sometimes makes you feel like the world is ending? You don't, and so I told a lot of quiet lies, reassuring and distracting her. When she finally hung up, I stayed sitting where I was, feeling too tired and tangled up to move.

Things never just end, do they? Every painful thing comes back to haunt you, time and time and time again.

I made myself move again and went back to finish transferring the old catalogue system to a digital form and set to checking the actual contents of the library against it. My enthusiasm was gone, so, deciding I had earned a change of pace, I allowed myself half an hour to poke around the small museum. This would need packing up too, with extra care and possibly some different-sized crates. There wasn't much there, and I couldn't help wondering if it wouldn't be better kept somewhere other than the new college. There were several military museums around Aldershot, and some of what was held here might be of interest to the regimental museums as well.

The slightly moth-eaten stuffed bulldog probably wasn't going anywhere, though. I wiped the dust off his laminated sign to find he was called, predictably enough, Winston, and had been a college mascot in the 1970s. I patted his head gingerly and said, "Sorry, boy." Next to him was a case of slightly rust-stained WWI medical instruments—at least I hoped it was rust—and a row of what looked like torpedoes below a competently executed watercolour of the hall. A mannequin in a WWII medical uniform took up the corner, next to a tabletop model of a dressing station beneath a whole wall full of photos of pre-

WWII graduating classes and rugby teams, all sitting with the same stiff-backed formality, their hair carefully Brylcreemed.

A large board had been leaned precariously against the wall, and a quick look told me this was the roll of honour. It showed signs of having been recently and carefully removed from a wall somewhere, so I guessed they'd put it in here for safekeeping. I shifted it carefully to a safer spot, revealing more pictures, laminated information sheets, and a sturdy wooden chest that looked older than anything else in here. A quick skim told me that the pages were a history of the hall before the Army took over, so I peeled them away from their ossified Blu-Tack and went to read them in the comfort of the main library.

The house was Jacobean, they informed me, although the gardens had been redone by Capability Brown, who was responsible for the lake. It had passed through the hands of three families and been notable for its library in the 1830s. It had been requisitioned as a hospital in WWI and, after the death of the last son of the family at Passchendaele, had passed into the Army's possession. A handful of well-known men had stayed or studied there, and a minor romantic poet had once spent a couple of years as the baronet's secretary. He was quoted at length.

The final paragraph informed me that the hall had no less than fourteen ghosts, including both a Grey Lady and a White Lady.

"What's wrong with Pink Ladies," I muttered. My bad dreams had faded by then, and I was feeling a little silly about how spooked I'd been. No wonder there were ghost stories about this place, if the boards creaked like that every night. Chuck in a wuthering gale and centuries-old windows, and it was a surprise there weren't *forty* ghosts associated with the place.

The fact sheets finished up with the information that the chest was a replica of one brought back from Italy by an earlier baronet, probably in the 1770s, who had been told that it was the original chest from the story of the Mistletoe Bride. The earl had supposedly imported the poor girl's ghost along with the chest, and she now wandered the halls as the White Lady of Eelmoor. I'd heard of the Mistletoe Bride before, and as she was also supposed to haunt at least three other places in Hampshire, two in Yorkshire, one in Cheshire, and possibly more that I didn't know about, I wasn't too convinced. Her story was all too clearly an early type of urban myth, attached to any building large and old enough to make the punchline faintly plausible. Schools—even medical schools—and ghost stories were a natural match.

I'd forgotten to ask McBride what time he finished work, but it was easy enough to watch out for his lights. When I saw them swing across the library windows, I gave it five minutes before I phoned his extension.

"Hey, I'm just finishing up for the day. You still want food?"

After a moment, he said, "Dr Alcott?"

"Who else is going to be calling on an internal line?"

"Fair point. Can you give me forty minutes?"

"Perfect timing. I was going to use the ground-floor kitchen by the library, so—"

"Power's off in there. Use yours."

"But—" I started cautiously, but he'd hung up. Well, he surely knew his own limitations. I wouldn't have wanted to tackle the staircases in here with an artificial leg, but it was his choice. Shrugging, I went round the library, locking up the museum and shutting down the computer. As I climbed up the gallery stairs, the lights below began to click off, the darkness growing steadily deeper. I was glad to step out into my bit of hallway. The little kitchen was warm and bright in comparison, just small enough to feel cosy. I stuck my laptop on a chair, put some music on, and set to work.

I was so absorbed that I didn't hear McBride approaching. I jumped about a foot when he suddenly said, "Smells good."

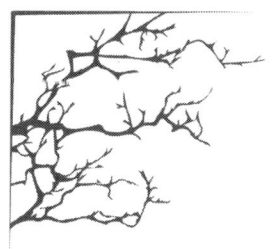

Chapter Four

"Thanks," I said when my nerves had settled. He had come bearing a six-pack, like any good guest. "Cardamom in the rice. Appreciate the beer."

His mouth twitched a little at the corner. "Who says it's for you?"

"See if I go easy on the heat for you now."

His eyes narrowed slightly. "Go easy? On me?"

"Oh, you want a challenge, then?" I grinned at him and was pleasantly gratified when he passed me a beer.

He cracked his own open and looked me up and down. "Asking for trouble, Professor? Had a few dodgy takeaways at your nice uni, did you? Think that makes you hard?"

"Now he talks," I said, grinning. "Scared you can't take the heat, soldier boy? Bet you ate a lot of rice pudding in the—what regiment?"

"Irish Guards." He folded his arms and glared.

"Up the Micks!" I said, not without respect. "Come on, then." I brought the chopping board and my pile of little green chilies round to the table beside him. "If I was being nice, it would be one per person. So, two each?"

"Three," he said, and took another slow sip of his beer as I chopped and added them.

"Chicken? Or are you veggie?"

"Meat's fine."

"But you'd prefer it freshly shot and gnawed straight from the bone?"

"If you're serving mammoth. Anything else, I'll compromise." He was giving me that half smile again, and I grinned back. Having company in my kitchen was going to my head. I'd cooked for Mark and Ciara a few times over the years, but less so since they'd had the girls. Friends, I met out; family, I went to. Just this tiny little luxury of having someone share my space, even a near stranger I wasn't sure I liked, was heady.

Yes, I was a bit of a sad bastard.

It was probably that sense of glee that made me say, as I passed McBride a plate full of food, "First one to drink is the loser?"

"Sure," he drawled, and we both pushed our open cans into the middle of the table.

One mouthful was enough to tell me that six chilies had been three too many. The only way I could tell whether I had chicken or rice in my mouth was by texture, and it burned its way down. Nonetheless, I said nonchalantly, "So, how was the assassination business today?"

"Busy," he said, taking his third forkful a little more slowly. "Icy roads."

"Makes me glad I don't drive anymore."

"But you did? Once?"

"Yup." I ate some more, trying to ignore the tears trickling down my cheeks. "Used to be a delivery driver for this Thai place in Balham while I was doing my masters."

He narrowed his eyes at me, which was impressive for someone slowly turning purple, and said admiringly, "Git."

"I ate a lot of cancelled orders that year," I said airily, but I had to take a breath before my next mouthful.

"I've eaten biryani in Basra."

"Really?"

"Yup. Don't get much heat in Iraqi food, though. Or Afghan stuff. They use spices for flavour, not heat."

That was fascinating, but I have to admit that I just smirked at him. "You're free to drink if you want to."

"Funny." He took another huge mouthful, and I followed, despite the slight concern that I couldn't quite feel the tip of my tongue or back of my throat anymore. "What type of chilies were they?"

"Bird's eye, I think. They weren't labelled, just the cheapest ones in that place by the station. I bought about a hundred for ten pence."

He grunted at me.

I took another mouthful.

So did he.

I said, "Did you know this place was haunted?"

"Heard some stories."

Another slow fork load each, and I was sure I wasn't the only one eyeing my drink with longing.

"It's even got a chest for the Mistletoe Bride."

"Who?"

I waved my fork at him. "Haven't you heard this one? Proper Victorian favourite, this. They used to stand up and recite it on Christmas afternoon. Basically, this poor girl got married on Christmas Eve, and after the wedding feast, they all decided to play hide-and-seek, as you do. Nobody could find her, and after a few days they just decided that she'd run off. Then, fifty years later, someone opens up a chest in the attic and finds her, still in her wedding dress and clutching a bit of mistletoe. Supposedly she'd hidden in there and the lid had fallen shut, and she couldn't get out."

"Bloody hell."

"Doesn't bear thinking about," I agreed, daring another mouthful. "Poor kid. They married young, back in the day, and she probably wasn't much more than a teenager."

McBride shuddered. "This happened here?"

"It's a legend. I know tons of places that claim it. This is just one of them."

"Think it's true?"

"No," I said. "It's all a bit too convenient, the wedding and the mistletoe and the oak chest. I wouldn't be surprised if it had its roots in some older folktale."

"It sounds plausible."

"That's why it's so effective. It's an urban myth, really." We'd both put down our forks, so I added casually, "If I count to five and we both drink, we could call it a draw."

"I will if you do."

"Scout's honour."

I counted up carefully, and on five we both lunged for our beer. It wasn't until we'd both drained half a can that I caught McBride's eye.

And he laughed.

It was a rough, low laugh, but it transformed him. Suddenly he wasn't grim, but alight with mischief and delight. The corners of his mouth lifted, his eyes brightened, and his cheeks rounded. Suddenly, for the first time that night, it struck me that I was sharing my meal with a man who was handsome, brave, and gay.

It flustered me enough that I jumped to my feet. "I've got some yogurt in the fridge. Want some?"

"Please." He grimaced faintly. "That was a stupid teenage stunt."

"Yeah, well, we've both proved we're real men," I babbled. "Even if we're not nineteen anymore."

"You can't be much more."

"Yeah, right," I said amicably. "I'm thirty-two."

He shot me a sceptical look.

"Honest. I've got myself a PhD and an honest job and own my flat, for the time being at least."

"Yeah?"

It wasn't much of an invitation to carry on, but I'd decided now that McBride wasn't so much an antisocial arse as severely unpractised at small talk. Possibly the beer and his smile had helped soften my attitude, but it was enough that I kept talking. I like having someone to bounce ideas off, and I'd had a few too many years with no one to talk to but myself, so I probably babbled. (Jay, reading over my shoulder right now, says I definitely did.)

He didn't talk back much, but he allowed himself the odd one-word comment, so I was sure he was listening. I wasn't quite sure why, since I was getting increasingly flustered by the very thereness of him (and, yes, I know that's not a word, but it's still the best way I can describe his presence). It's odd, looking back, but I think even then I was sensing that essential quality. Jay isn't articulate, or romantic, but he is the most reliable person I have ever known. Once he has your back, you can trust him absolutely, and he has never let me dow—

Okay, I'm going to let that stand. Somebody took a simple statement of fact as being a bit provocative, and things got a little out of hand.

He's sleeping beside me now, his face pressed against my side. It's hard to type when I keep having to reach down and touch his hair, smoothing out the tangles and brushing it away from his face. There's grey in it now that wasn't there during that first meal we shared (silver amongst the gold, I'd say, but I can just imagine how he'd grimace at that). He looks better now, less brittle and angry, still utterly himself, but easier about it. We were a right pair of lost souls, there in Eelmoor Hall.

Three lost souls, if you count her.

He's stirring now, his eyelashes flaring and his mouth moving. He's pressing his forehead against my skin, breathing in, murmuring something that might be my name.

"Still writing your ghost story?" he's just asked, pulling himself up, throwing his leg over mine, and lolling against my shoulder.

You're making it hard to type, gorgeous, and this bit isn't a ghost story. It's about how wonderful you are.

Yes, I am a sentimental fool. You love me for it.

Oh, I'm sorry. Am I embarrassing you? I quite like it, putting these things down in words, making them concrete. Shall I tell you more? I love the way you pretend not to find my jokes funny but can't quite hide your smile. I love the satisfaction you get from riding to the rescue, even if you call half the drivers you help idiots. I love that you would never think of making yourself a cup of tea without making me one too, the way you steal the duvet right back and usually drag me along with it, your morning growls. I love your shoulders, how strong they are and how they flex under my hands when I'm holding on tight, when I'm riding you.

You're breathing fast against my neck. I can tell you like this.

So shall we keep going?

I'll take that grunt as a yes.

I like your mouth, the way it looks hard and tastes soft. I like that spot above your stump, the one that makes you gasp every time I touch it. I like the hair on your belly, how I feel it against my knuckles every time I jerk you off.

I like it when you kiss the side of my neck.

Lower.

There.

When you pinch my nipples.

I'm hard for you again. Go on. Lift the sheet. See for yourself.

Can't type if you touch me like that.

No, don't stop. Tell me what I get if I put this thing down.

Really? Okay, then.

Jay thinks I should delete that now it's morning. I'd rather keep it for posterity. The good memories are worth preserving. When we're old and limp dicked in some nursing home somewhere, we can read over this and fondly remember the good old days.

Perhaps that's why I'm writing this, after all. Perhaps it's not just for me. After all, we were both there.

Oh, and for the record, we didn't have sex that first night. McBride put up with my wittering, did the washing up, and disappeared back to his own rooms. I sat up and read in bed for a bit, but I couldn't really concentrate. McBride had me intrigued. It was nice to have something to speculate about that wasn't related to my own dramas, and I couldn't help wondering what his story was. I wasn't attracted to him at that point, beyond the general awareness that he was hot, but he was interesting, and it had been a very long time since I let myself be interested.

I was still thinking about him when I drifted off to sleep.

That night I dreamed of Danny, dreamed he was here with me, striding along the corridors of Eelmoor Hall ahead of me, flinging the doors open with delight and shouting to me to come and see what he'd found. With every step, he drew further ahead, and when I tried to catch up, I found myself lost in a tangle of rooms, his voice echoing around me.

I woke up some hours later, paralyzed again. I fought it, trying to lash out. My body wouldn't answer, and this time it was worse. This time, the air felt tight and heavy around me, pressing against my sides. I couldn't breathe properly. It felt like someone had drained all the oxygen from the room.

Just as I was starting to hyperventilate, the fear came again, rolling over me in cold waves.

I struggled to move, to get away. I failed, and the darkness only seemed to grow tighter and heavier around me.

Eventually, like the first night, it faded, leaving me sweating and cramped. And again I heard footsteps.

This time they weren't upstairs. This time they were in the hallway outside. I knew it wasn't McBride.

I lost count of how many times they passed my door, but eventually they moved away, fading into the distance, and didn't return.

I could move then, but I didn't. I just lay in the dark and shuddered.

I WAS UP EARLY AGAIN, but this time I needed to get out of the damn building. As soon as it was light enough, I went out for a run.

It was a lovely morning, sharp with frost, and the ground crunched under my feet. I followed the gravel path along the side of the main garden and turned off to follow the track around the lake. The edges of the lake had frozen, and ferns rose out of the yellowed heath on my other side, glittering with frost. I startled a deer, who went leaping into the woods, and a few moments later, a heron, who went coasting out over the lake on broad wings.

By the time I made it into the complex of modern buildings behind the main house, my nerves had settled.

I came across McBride as he exited one of the newer buildings. He raised his hand in greeting. "Morning, Dr Alcott."

"Morning, Sergeant McBride," I said back smartly.

He glared at me. "Jay."

I pointed at myself. "Nope, I'm Luke, remember?"

That got a quirk of his mouth.

"You off to work already?"

"Yeah. Different shift." He cleared his throat a little awkwardly. "So, dinner."

"Sorry. Bit toxic in the end, wasn't it?"

"No. Tonight's dinner." At my blank look, he added, "Here. Owe you one."

"Oh. Love to."

"Right. Seven."

"On the dot," I agreed. "Enjoy your day."

Running back towards the hall, I found myself thinking pleasantly, *Jay McBride.*

I had a good day, my work only interrupted by an easy lunchtime walk to the shop in the next village for beer and extra chocolate Hobnobs (heaving around files is hungry work). The frost was still lingering in the more wooded stretches of the heath, under the dark pines and the bare arches of the birches, and the sky was that clear, blazing blue you only get on a fine midwinter's day. An occasional airplane went roaring overhead, taking off from Farnborough Airport on the far side of the canal. There were soldiers training, stumbling by with packs on their backs as they ran, their faces flushed and their breath rising in pale clouds. I took a detour to walk along part of Long Valley, where

60,000 troops had once mustered to celebrate Queen Victoria's Golden Jubilee. These days it's used more by off-road bikers, but the memories of more glorious times linger. There's something very pleasing about walking through a place and knowing the history of the ground beneath your feet, and I enjoyed the walk.

It was good to get back, though. I found myself letting out a satisfied sigh when Eelmoor Hall rose back into sight. The sun was falling onto the south face by then, lighting up the bay windows and making the brickwork look warm and bright. It's not often you get to work somewhere with so much history, and I found myself appreciating it. I returned to the work with excitement, and by the time evening came round again and I headed off to dinner with Jay, ghosts were the last thing on my mind.

Jay lived in one of the old instructors' dorms, not the main hall. It was modern and scruffy, the corner unit in one of these weirdly spiky seventies blocks you usually only find in universities and other public edifices. The modern part of the site was bigger than I'd realized, and my footsteps echoed a little too loudly for comfort as I walked through it. There's something very unnerving about an empty college, something about all the glass and concrete and big rooms full of silence behind every door.

Jay's two rooms felt much cosier than the echoing hallways of the main house, though. He had a big kitchen, all done up in brown Formica and furniture so resolutely plain that it must have been bought in bulk by a procurement officer who had never actually lived in barracks housing.

Jay turned out to be a pretty good cook, and we spent another easy evening together. He let slip some stories about his deployments, and I chattered back. It wasn't until the end of the evening, when I got up to clear away our plates, that he suddenly said, "What happened to your knuckles?"

"Woke up like that," I said ruefully. They had been reddened and bleeding that morning.

"You hit something in your sleep?"

"I'm clumsy," I admitted, shrugging. "Danny always used to say I had a genius for breaking the unbreakable." And I stopped, because I'd managed not to mention Danny yet.

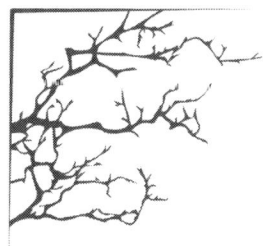

Chapter Five

"Danny?"

"My ex," I said and looked down at my hands. My battered knuckles were safer than Jay's face.

"Recent?"

"Complicated," I said back. I had a set explanation for this, one I could recite without my voice catching. I closed my eyes and reeled it off. "We met at uni and moved in together when we graduated. I was doing my masters, and Danny was training for the bar. He disappeared on the tenth of April, 2005. He took his wallet, but not his phone or passport. He left one message on his brother's phone, but never contacted us again. He never came back. Technically the police investigation is still open, but it's not active." I opened my eyes to see Jay regarding me steadily and added, "This week I decided to put our flat on the market."

"Hard decision."

"Yeah." I grimaced. "Even the world's greatest optimist has to give up in the end."

"Nothing wrong with optimism. Police ever find any leads?"

"Nothing that went anywhere. Shit, I think *I* was their best lead."

"You wouldn't hurt someone you loved." It was said as flatly as any fact, but it startled me. Even Mark hadn't had quite that much faith in me.

"Luckily, my motive was also my alibi." Without intending to, I reached up and touched the lump in my nose.

"He did that?"

"He had a problem with drink. And drugs. Addiction in general, really, but the drink was the main thing. There was work stress too, and coming out messed up a lot of things for him."

"A lot of people have bad stories. They don't take it out on their partners."

"It wasn't his fault," I said. Nobody ever believed me about this. "He was a good guy. It wasn't really part of him, the anger and the hurt. It was an illness, or something that was in him that gave way under all that pressure. He needed help." And I hadn't got it for him, hadn't realized how bad it was until we were already drowning. "It's like... he always drank a bit too much, see, but not to the point that anyone thought he had a problem. Couple of nights when we were undergrads where he threw up in someone's hedge, got a firm telling-off from a police officer once after he tried to unlock the wrong bike from the rack on Gloucester Green and got a bit rowdy. Stuff that a lot of people do, y'know. And then his parents tell him to get out and never come back, and it was like dropping a glass on the kitchen floor. Sometimes it's fine, and sometimes it just lands all wrong, hits in that one spot that makes it shatter." I stopped, forcing myself to take a breath. I'd spent a lot of time trying to explain it to myself, so if that sounded like it was a bit pat, that's why. You get a lot of time to hone your metaphors in the long years after the shit hits the fan.

"Met a few guys with PTSD when I was...." He paused and then continued wryly, "Recovering. It was like someone had put a cloud inside their heads. Even they couldn't see who they really were."

"Yeah," I said. "Like that."

I was feeling grateful until he asked, "So, how did him breaking your nose give you an alibi?"

"Hit my head on the way down. Last thing he did was get me to casualty. They kept me in for observation for a few nights, by which time Mark—that's his brother—was raising hell."

"You're not angry with him," Jay observed.

"Most of the world would tell me I was wrong."

"It's your anger."

I looked up at him, startled. "Yeah, it is. Sorry, got a bit grim there. How about a more cheerful topic? Got any ideas what I label the stash of dodgy mags in my archive? I can't decide if they go under Periodicals, Illustrated, or Ephemera."

He let me change the subject. "How about, 'Just look on the top shelf, lads.'"

"Might stick that in the front on a Post-it note."

I wandered back to the main house later in a more sombre frame of mind. It was rare to tell that story to someone who didn't immediately jump to judgment. Jay hadn't liked what Danny had done, but he hadn't called me a fool, either. Too many people took it as a chance to lecture me on my self-worth, lack of self-preservation, or naïveté.

It's amazing how many people think I'm a victim, or a martyr. None of them ever seem to consider that I was, just like Danny, making desperate choices in a bad situation. It was never about me. I was collateral damage in his self-destruction. I *chose* to be part of that fight. Whatever people assume, I was never passive, and I don't need them to critique my decisions as if I'm too feeble to think for myself. Maybe it would have been right for them to walk away.

But I stayed.

Until now, that was, and that was on my mind as I fell asleep.

Unsurprisingly, I dreamed that Danny came back. In the dream he was already dead, sitting beside my bed with a pallid face and blue lips. "You should have looked," he kept saying. "You should have kept looking."

I tried to answer, but he reached out and touched me with his cold, clammy hands, pressing his palm over my mouth. I couldn't breathe, and I fought to throw him off. He was immovable, though, his sunken eyes turned towards me in silent reproach.

"You were supposed to look for me," he said as I struggled to breathe, clawing at his hand. "You were supposed to keep looking."

Darkness closed around him, and I woke. I was ready for the fear and paralysis this time, though I still tried to fight it. I had a growing conviction that giving in would make it worse, that the nights would grow colder and darker and the weight that pressed me to the bed would get heavier.

This time, when it faded, there were no footsteps outside the door.

They were in the room, and I could hear the stiff rustle of silk brushing against the floor between the bed and window, slow and steady. I strained to see through the darkness, but I couldn't even see movement—could just hear that relentless *tap-rustle*, *tap-rustle* of her passing.

When dawn broke through the window and I was free to move again, I lifted my throbbing hands and saw that I'd done more than scrape my knuckles this time. My nails were torn and my palms bleeding, as if I had clawed all night at the walls.

I thought myself round in circles all day. I might not believe in ghosts, but three times is still enemy action, whether you believe in it or not. The question was whether the enemy was the Ghost of Eelmoor Hall (unlikely) or whether it was my own subconscious finally falling over that last edge (probable). It didn't help that I kept hearing that slow *creak-creak* of steps outside the door, or that it stopped dead every time I noticed and tried to focus on it. I knew it was just the natural noises of an old house on a cold, damp day, and that all ghost stories rose out of the power of the human imagination and our minds' inclination to create a story out of random incidents.

Every time I got lost in my own thoughts, however, the automatic lights eventually clicked off, and I knew that I was not alone.

Why was I so certain?

I could hear her breathing.

You may well be asking at this point why I didn't just run like hell. The best explanation I have is that you get locked into a certain type of stubbornness, partly "you can't beat me, bitch" and partly "if I run, it's real," and the longer you stay the harder it is to leave.

Look, I didn't say it was a *good* reason.

Each time the lights went out, it felt harder and harder to move to bring them back. It wasn't so much that I was afraid of what I might see, as that I was afraid of what might see me. In the dark, we were both hiding.

Then Jay came in, setting the lights off, and the sound of breathing stopped. He took one look at me where I was hunched in the in the desk chair and said, "What happened?"

"Nothing," I said, finally moving. "Spooked myself."

His eyes narrowed and he came towards me, not quickly but steadily. "And your hands?"

I looked down at them. "Bad dreams again."

"Can give you a hand moving the bed away from the wall."

"Actually, only the head's against the wall, but thanks for the offer."

"Then how did you do that to yourself?"

I looked up at him, startled, and said slowly, "That's actually a very good question." All that time I'd been trying to fight back, I'd been unable to move. Why *were* my hands bloodied?

"Talk."

I sighed, putting my hands back on my knees where he couldn't see them. "You'll think I'm mad. I think I'm mad. I don't even believe in ghosts."

"I do."

That surprised me. "Really?"

"Yup." He pushed my chair back and scowled down at my hands. "You put anything on those?"

"I cleaned them," I said, suddenly aware all over again of his physicality, my body suddenly tensing with his nearness. "It's only scratches."

"Bandages." He clarified at my puzzled expression. "You need some, working in here with all this dust."

I laughed. "Don't even notice it."

"Stay here." He turned to head out and then paused and came back. "Second thoughts. You're done for the day."

"I've got an awful lot more to do."

"Getting much done at the moment, are you?"

I looked at the screensaver swirling on my laptop, considered how often the lights had gone out in the last few hours, and shrugged. "Fair enough."

He dragged me up to my kitchen in the lift and took a first aid kit I hadn't found yet out from under the sink. He made me wash the scratches out again, applied copious amounts of antiseptic cream, and reached for bandages. I demurred at that. I wasn't averse to having a strong man forcefully tend my wounds, but that was overkill.

"Intending to wreck your hands again tonight?" he said.

"Of course not."

"Intend to the last two nights?"

"No," I said and then caught his point.

"So we cover them up so you don't make this worse. Now talk."

"It doesn't make sense," I said and pulled my hands back. "And I'm not putting those on until I absolutely have to. I can't hold a pen in them. Or a fork."

He sighed heavily and went to survey the contents of the fridge. With his back to me, he said, "When I first got back to the UK, to the military ward up in Birmingham, there was a lad in the next bed. Jack. Cheery lad. He'd lost his right foot; made all the usual jokes. Asked the doctor if he'd ever be able to dance again, all that. Told me he'd been caught when a mine went off at Wipers.

Didn't want to talk about it, which was fine by me. Talked about his girl instead. His dog. His mum, who worked in a factory up north somewhere, and how worried she was. Next morning, I woke up and he was gone. So was the bed he'd been in." He paused, shaking his head a little. "Didn't think Wipers sounded like somewhere in the sandbox, but I don't speak French, let alone Farsi. It was only when I asked the nurses about him that I found out—"

"Ypres," I said, suddenly working it out. "In the Great War, the soldiers called Ypres Wipers."

"Yeah. Turns out Jack never got home to his mum, poor bastard. Gangrene. 1915. Nurses knew all about him. Said he turns up from time to time. Cheers up the newcomers, if he can."

I breathed in slowly, looking at him. From anyone else, it might have sounded unlikely, but he was so matter of fact about it, and I'd yet to see any evidence he was a liar.

"Now your ghost," he said, getting chicken out.

"What are you doing?"

"Cooking."

"It's my turn."

"I'll cook. You talk."

Well, what would you have done, dear reader? I told him everything.

And yeah, all right, reader, I married him too, but not that evening or even that year. It takes time to build something this solid, you know. It had its foundations there, I think, in that evening when he said more than I'd ever heard from him in one go, just so I would doubt myself less. I remember sitting there, watching his steady competence as he cooked and listened to me spill out all my night fears, and thinking to myself, *Oh, you're a good one, Jay McBride.*

When I finished, he nodded thoughtfully and said, "Reckon it's your girl in the chest?"

"The Mistletoe Bride? Why?"

He shrugged. "You mentioned her. Got her attention, maybe."

"No, it started before that. First night I was here."

"What does she want?"

"Does she have to want anything?" I asked. "Maybe she just likes torturing people." I thought better of it. "No, you're right. There'd be a lot more than a line of text in the museum if this happened to everyone who lived here, or even everyone who used that room. Unless it's been left unused?"

"No. Standard study bedroom. That's how the stories go, right? They want something. Ghosts."

"What did Jack want?" For a moment, I regretted asking. It had been a private story, and I didn't want him to think I was prying.

"Someone to talk to," he said. "Bit of company. What anyone wants, if they're safe otherwise."

"I really don't think she wanted a conversation," I said. "Although I dreamed Danny did. He was angry that I wasn't still looking...."

I trailed off as Jay swung round to face me. "Tell me someone found her. The girl in the chest."

"In the story? Yeah, her dad in some versions, her aged husband in others."

"So she's not still in the bloody box?"

I shook my head. "Not in the story, but I'm not sure it's the physical box that matters most with things like that. God, can you imagine how it must have felt—trapped in there, in the dark, hearing everyone give up on looking? She must have been so afraid."

"You think?" Jay said. "Me, I'd have been angry."

"Angry?"

"Just married, wasn't she? He'd made her promises and then left her there to die in a box."

I shuddered. "Oh, God, you think she knows? That I gave up on Danny?"

He busied himself with serving food, clattering the pans loudly. Once we were both sitting down, he said, very clearly and carefully, "You didn't give up on your bloke. He gave up on you."

"I should have—"

"No. *He* should have. Eat your dinner and talk about something else until you're done."

"Who needs a mother, with you around?" I muttered, but I did as I was told.

After dinner he came back to what we had both been circling. "She's chasing you. You should leave."

I shrugged. "I'm not worried. Come on, aren't you curious? Don't you want to know what she's after?" Warm food and human company had taken the edge off my nerves, and I thought I could get through a few more waking nightmares before my curiosity deserted me completely.

"No."

"Not even a little bit?"

"There's a saying. About a cat. You might know it."

"Never understood that one myself. Nobody's ever actually died of curiosity, have they? They don't write it on death certificates."

"Maybe. Maybe not. Stupidity, though, that kills a lot of people."

"Hey." I fiddled with my fork, trying to catch the last few grains of rice, and said, without meeting his eyes, "Maybe it's my job to stay."

"Get hazard pay as a professor? Going to pack up the ghost in a box between the titty mags and Winston the Mouldy Dog?"

"You know about Winston?"

"Everyone who's ever worked here knows about Winston. He's lucky. Don't change the subject."

I shrugged and got up to clear the plates away. Looking out of the window, where the night was so dark all I could see was my own reflection, I quoted, "'See! the old man weeps for his fairy bride.' That's from the old song. In the story, at least, he did look, and he still missed her years later. How many people who come here are going to get that?"

"Still doesn't make it your problem."

"I think maybe it does."

Jay let out a long irritated sigh. "Talk it through." He says that a lot, though that was the very first time. He claims that for someone who talks so much, I get lost in my own head too easily. I admit, for the first few years, I used to just present him with faits accomplis, ideas about both of us that I'd reasoned through and refined all by myself. It took a while to realize why it annoyed him, and much longer to stop doing it. Even now, it's a rare week that he doesn't have to remind me. *Talk it through, Luke, bit by bit.*

"What if it was Danny? What if there was something he wanted to tell me—us—and this was the only way he could? I don't think I could forgive the person who refused to listen to him."

"This isn't your Danny."

The thought hadn't occurred to me until then. "How do we know that? He was in my dream. It could be him. It could be—"

"Luke! Look at your hands!" It was the first time he'd raised his voice, even slightly, and it jerked me out of my rising panic.

"My hands?"

He took them, turning them over so I could see the damage to my knuckles. He had strong hands, but he was gentle with them. "There," he said. "That. If you were hitting the inside of a box, if you were trapped in one, you'd bust your hands up just like that."

I shuddered. "Probably not Danny, then. Damn."

Jay was looking at me with that unreadable, considering expression again. "Tell me something about him. Something good."

How? How could I pick out just one thing to explain Danny in all his casual brilliance? I'd seen him drunk and happy, flirting his way through a club but always coming back to me. I'd watched countless times as he held a door or ran to help someone with a heavy bag, and then, if it happened to be a girl and she took it as flirting, he would stroll back to me, shove his hand in my back pocket, and wink at her. I'd seen him tussle with Mark without letting slip he'd been boasting about his amazing little brother for three days before he arrived. He could quote most of *The Princess Bride* off by heart. He'd moaned about my cold feet in bed and then bought me a pair of ridiculous bed socks with cartoon willies on them. He'd always bought the first and last rounds.

"He was kind," I said at last. "Funny. He'd act like this big cocky joker, but he was decent underneath. When we were students, our female friends never had to walk home alone when it was late, not if he was sober enough to go with them. He'd joke around and wind them up so they wouldn't notice, but he'd do it all the way to their front door. Used to piss some of them off once they caught on. He...." I tried to find the right words. "He was just Danny. He was a person, not a problem. I wish people would remember that."

"You do." He was still holding my hands, and I was suddenly very aware of it. He was just a little taller than me, but broader. He looked like someone you could lean on, though I was conscious of his leg. For the first time, I wasn't just aware of him. I was actively imagining what it would be like to have him hold me, to lift my mouth to his kiss, to grab those broad shoulders and pull myself close to him.

"Still need to bandage those hands," he said, and there was just enough softness in his voice to make me look up. His face was still expressionless, but there was enough heat in his eyes to make me catch my breath. I swayed forward, and he breathed in hard.

And above us, there was a soft creak. We both froze as it was repeated and then became the familiar sound of footsteps.

"That's her," I breathed.

"Shit." Jay blew out hard, and he was close enough that I felt it brush my cheek.

"Guess I'm not crazy, then," I said.

"Never doubted you. Something else to hear it for myself." He frowned suddenly. "Although we've not once considered that it might *not* be a ghost."

"In my bedroom? Not triggering the light sensors?"

"Sounds carry." He stepped back. "I'm obliged to check."

"You're going up there?"

"Could be someone looking for a dry place to sleep. Bit far out of town, though."

"I'm coming with you."

He gave me a dirty look, and I don't mean the good kind of dirty. "I'm capable."

"I believe you, but did you not watch any horror movies in the Army? *Never* go off and explore the haunted house on your own."

"Fine." I got a quirk of his mouth for it, though. "What could possibly go wrong?"

We took the lift up to the second floor. When we stepped out, the corridor was dark and silent. I waved my hand through the air to trigger the lights, but nothing happened. Jay stepped out past me, muttering, "Duff sensor, maybe," and walked a few steps along the corridor.

Still no light, and now I heard a faint sound at the end of the corridor. I stepped forward quickly, wanting to be closer to Jay, and collided with him.

"Careful."

"Listen."

The sound was clear now. Somebody was walking towards us through the darkness.

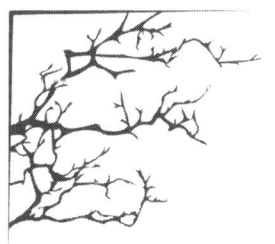

Chapter Six

Jay swore, and I felt him wrestling something off his belt. A moment later, a light clicked on as he swung his torch across the breadth of the corridor.

There was no one there, just closed doors and folding chairs stacked against the wall, but the steps kept coming closer and closer. If I'd been alone, I would have dived into the lift and huddled in the corner until she went away, but Jay wasn't moving, so I didn't either. We both stood there like stupid macho lumps as the footsteps drew closer and closer with a soft rustle of silk against the polished floor.

They stopped, and in the stillness, I heard her breathing right in front of us. My hand was still resting against Jay's leg, and my fist twisted up slowly, clenching in the loose fabric of his jeans tightly enough that I could feel the cool, rigid side of his prosthetic through the denim.

Then she moved, rushing past us so quickly that I felt her skirt brush over my leg. Her steps faded past us, further along the hallway.

"That would be a ghost, then," Jay said. "Luke?"

"Yeah?" I wasn't managing nonchalant quite so convincingly, and my voice wobbled.

"I can't get back in the lift until you let go of my jeans."

"Right." I unclenched my fist and he grabbed my hand instead, pulling me back into the safety of the bright cube of the lift. He didn't let go until we were back in the kitchen, where he sank down in a chair with a sigh. I managed to stagger over to the counter to grab the last two beers and then sat down beside him, so close our knees were touching.

"I need fucking hard liquor after that," he muttered and then looked straight at me. "Don't sleep in your own bed tonight."

I think my whole body lit up at once. All I could think was, *I need that. I need someone to push me down and make me come until I don't care if the bloody ghost is watching. I need this man to do it.*

My reaction must have been obvious, because Jay blushed, a sudden flush that rose up from his chin to his forehead in one bright wave. "Uh. I didn't mean. There's room in the other houses. My sofa."

Well, damn.

Then he added, a little diffidently, "Not that I *wouldn't*, mind. Just not what I meant. Didn't want you to think I was—"

"Any time," I said, and I spread my hand over his thigh in case he hadn't got the message. "Now, for instance."

He swallowed hard, covering my hand with his own. "And our invisible neighbour?"

"The one with probable abandonment issues?" I asked, closing my eyes. "Shit."

"I don't want her to hurt you."

I opened my eyes. "What's she going to do? Seriously, she's dead, which is sad and all that, but—"

He lifted my hand and pressed a kiss just above my bloodied knuckles. "She's already made you bleed."

I swore quite a lot. "Fine. Then I'm staying here tonight."

His look got a lot less tender. "If you don't want my sofa, there's a Travelodge in town."

"No, thanks. I've still got at least two weeks' work to do, and she's not going to go away. If she does want something, moving out will only slow that process down, and you've just given me a damn good incentive to end it quickly."

His glare hardened.

"No, look—it makes perfect sense. She started talking to me through my dreams last night. Maybe she'll tell me what she wants tonight."

"That's not sense."

"It's worth a try, though."

"I'm staying with you."

"Doesn't that rather defeat the—"

He kissed my knuckles again, featherlight. "You have a chair in your room, right?"

I gave him a glare of my own. "I do not need a nursemaid."

"Got one anyway."

The argument didn't end there, but eventually I found myself plodding across the lawns with Jay to fetch what he needed for the night. Back in his modern little kitchen with its little plastic Christmas tree and string of cheap tinsel over the window, ghosts seemed very unlikely again, and I relaxed with a sigh.

"Sure you don't want to stay?" he asked.

"Don't tempt me. You really think she can't see us here?"

"Never heard or felt anything here."

That would do. I crossed the room and cupped his cheek, pulling his mouth down to mine.

It was just a kiss, just a soft, slightly uncertain press of lips to lips, just a brush of tongue, just a sigh. There was no reason for my whole body to feel lighter when our mouths finally parted, no reason for my breath to catch, no reason for my heart to tighten.

"Yeah, this is going to be worth waiting for," I said a little stupidly, aware that Jay's arms were still folded tightly around me.

"Damn it, Luke." He kissed me again, and it was—you know when you've been outside so long that you don't even realize how hot and tired you are, and then you buy a cold drink, and that first mouthful just makes the whole world better?

Like that. Just like that.

"Should stop," he said. "While we can."

He left me standing there to get his stuff, and I leaned back against the kitchen counter, still a little light-headed. I'd slept with other men since Danny had gone, nameless bodies I'd met in clubs, always back to their place just in case, always gone by morning. Some of them had been hot, some had even been sweet, but none had ever been tender. Standing there, I touched my mouth and tried to remember the last time someone had treated me with tenderness.

"Luke." He was back, with a small backpack slung over his shoulder. "Let's go."

I followed him back through the staff housing and across the lawns. The clouds had parted and there was a sliver of a moon overhead, not enough to light our path. The stars were all the brighter without it, barely blurred by the orange glow of the towns on our horizons. I didn't know many constellations, but I looked up at them that night, finding the few I could recognize. Even I can spot Orion, for instance, striding out fiercely towards the little cluster of the Pleiades, always just out of his reach.

Back on the terrace, we both hesitated, loath to go inside. Jay stepped backwards into the shelter of the arcade, where we couldn't be overlooked. I went with him, and he kissed me quickly. "Still time to change your mind."

"No. Let's do this."

It was a bit of an anti-climax going back in. There were no more footsteps, and we managed to do the washing-up and convert the armchair in my room into something Jay could sleep in all night. I changed in the bathroom, and in case you're wondering, I didn't wear anything provocative or even forgo my shirt—firstly because we were trying not to piss off the ghost by having sex, and secondly because it was a seventeenth-century mansion in December, in a country that still regards efficient central heating as mildly immoral. I wore my fleece pj's, two pairs of socks, and a sweater on top of that, just like I had the last three nights.

Jay took one look at me and broke into laughter. "All you're missing is a bobble hat."

"I get cold," I said. "Seriously, don't you want more blankets?"

"Slept in worse places."

"Make me feel inadequate, why don't you?" I grumbled and scooted into bed, switching the main light off and the bedside lamp on as I passed them. Even the sheets were cold. "I don't feel in the least bit sleepy."

"Not going to tell you a bedtime story."

"Aww, and I was hoping for a lullaby."

He gave me the finger and I blew him a kiss, which only made him glare more. I was feeling silly and giddy, perhaps in reaction to the scare earlier, perhaps because this man had kissed me, and I wanted to make him smile, wanted to laugh with him even if we couldn't do anything else.

"Turn round."

"Why?" I said, eyeing him blatantly. "If you're planning to undress, don't feel shy."

He was quiet for a moment before he said flatly, "I have to charge my leg overnight. Battery won't last until morning."

"Go for it."

"I have to take it off first."

I didn't get it at first. "No problem."

"Luke." He swallowed hard, but his voice stayed steady. "I don't want you to see."

Oh. Without another word, I turned around, staring at the wall and wondering. The bed would be wide enough for two, if they were friendly, and I wondered if we'd made the wrong choice. The space between us seemed all the wider for being in the same room. To bridge it, I said quietly, "It wouldn't scare me off."

"Go to sleep, Luke."

"Tell me when I can turn round."

I heard him moving quietly for a little longer before he said, "Okay."

He'd pulled the blanket up to cover his legs and lap, but his prosthetic was standing by the chair, plugged into the wall with something that looked much like my phone charger. A little blue light shone near the base. Standing free like that, it looked like a very alien mechanism, modern in an old place. I'd written papers on military medicine, though, and read at length about the ongoing suffering of those who came home crippled from Crimea and Gallipoli and the Somme. To me, Jay's leg looked like a miracle.

He had already folded his arms and closed his eyes, so I reached up and turned the lamp out. "Goodnight."

I got a grunt in return, and before long I slipped into sleep as well, despite the lingering thrill of nervousness.

I WOKE SOME TIME LATER to the comforting sense of someone asleep on the bed behind me, arm loose across my waist and breathing steady in my ear. For a moment I thought it was Danny, and then I woke up enough to know better.

"Jay?" I tried to ask, but only the faintest sound came out. Yet again I was frozen in my sleep, and I realized suddenly that I could feel wood against my knuckles even though my hands were tucked under the covers. I made a louder noise, hoping to rouse him.

"Luke?" he said sleepily from the far side of the room.

Behind me, the breathing continued softly, stirring the hairs at the back of my neck.

I tried to scream, and as I did, the fear rose up over me as if I was being buried in ice from the toes up. My fingers curled up, my pulse quickened, sweat prickled on my shoulders, my back, my brow. It gripped me so hard I felt like I was convulsing, but I wasn't. I was still trapped into stillness, and my scream came out as a thin whistle.

"Luke?" Jay's voice seemed a world away, echoing strangely as if I were hearing him through a closed door.

Or the sides of a sturdy oak chest.

The fear receded, fading like an echo. Behind me, the cold breathing changed, becoming quicker and less even, and the arm over my waist moved, sliding up until I felt a chilly narrow hand press above my heart. Her breath moved across my neck, and a frail female voice, faintly accented, whispered forlornly into my ear, *"It's so cold in this box."*

"Luke!" Jay's torch came on, lighting up the room, and whatever he saw in my face had him jumping out of his chair. I saw the inevitable moment when he lost his balance, the lunge he made for the top of the chair, the torch flying out of his hands. In the twisting light I saw glimpses of him: pushing off the chair, falling towards the door, his empty trouser leg twisting beneath him.

The fear started again, and she sighed against my cheek, soft and triumphant.

The light came on so suddenly it stung my eyes. At once the fear vanished and so did she, as quick as a blink.

Jay was hanging on to the door frame, one hand pressed to the wall beside the switch.

I could move again, and I threw myself out of bed, landing hard with the duvet tangled around my feet. I kicked it off and stumbled over to Jay, getting my shoulder under his arm. He grabbed on hard, and I wasn't sure if it was more for balance or for a hug.

"Look!" he said, tipping his chin towards the bed. I looked and shuddered again. There were two dents in the mattress, one where I had been lying and the other behind it, refilling slowly.

"Did you hear?" I asked him. We were both breathing fast. "Did the fear get you too?"

"Yes." He took a long breath. "I don't care how curious you are—"

"Investigation's over," I agreed.

"Get the fuck out?"

"Oh, God, yes."

He nodded sharply. "Help me back over there."

I supported him to the chair, where he snapped, "Shoes, Luke."

"Yeah, okay, shit." I was still shaking.

"Hold it together, kid."

"Fuck off," I said automatically. "I'm probably older than you." It got me moving, though, and I shoved my shoes on with shaking fingers as Jay saw to his leg. I tried not to watch, but he was so quick and competent it steadied me a little, the careful slide of cloth and the click of metal, and the long slow beep of the power coming on. He was ready to move before I was.

We made it all the way down to the exit onto the terrace without a hint of anything supernatural. Then, as Jay laid his hand on the door, the floor creaked in the darkness at the far end of the hall, as it would under the press of a narrow foot.

We didn't wait around.

Jay had grabbed my hand on the way out and was trying to drag me across the lawns. Considering he couldn't go faster than a brisk walk and my panic was rapidly turning into the kind of nervous jitters that could have fuelled a run into town and back, it was more sweet than effective, but I had no intention of letting go.

The nerves came out in a babble of conversation and frantic glances back at the hall, now dark and brooding behind us. "Shit, we never locked the library. Do we need to go back?"

"No." Jay's hand tightened on mine. He was holding the torch steady ahead of us, its beam lighting the gravel path and catching on the frost in the grass.

"Have you got your key? I think I left mine."

"In my pocket."

We'd reached the steps down to the drive, and he let go of me, handing over the torch so he could negotiate the old stairs. I shone it on them, trying to keep my shaking hands steady, and wondered if she was watching too, standing right behind us. What if she pushed one of us? It wouldn't take much to have us both falling. Then we'd be lying out here in the cold all night, and neither of us was dressed for it.

"Shit, I'm still in my pj's. Seriously, you'd better have a key, because if I get hypothermia and die and end up haunting the place with her, I'll—"

"Your pyjamas could insulate a small Arctic research station." Jay was at the bottom of the steps, and he looked up, holding out his hand.

"I get cold," I complained, hurrying down to join him. "I mean, I'm sure that I'd acclimatize if I had to live out in the bloody countryside much longer, but—"

"Luke."

"Yeah?"

"Stop talking."

"Why?"

"So I can hear if she's coming after us."

I shut up at that point. Do you blame me? We stood there at the bottom of the steps, still and listening, and the panic jittering through me changed, settling tightly in my gut and around my heart.

There was no sound behind us but the slow sigh of the wind through the conifers, the bark of a fox, an owl's long cry. There were no footsteps on the gravel.

Jay waited longer than I would have done, long enough that I was starting to get restless, but at last he said, "Clear."

"I don't think she's going to shoot us."

"Keep walking, Luke."

"I'm walking. Just saying."

I was pretty sure the look he was giving me was less than fond. "You'd be a pain to rescue."

"Oh, is this a rescue now? I thought we were both just running away."

The drive was lined with tall dark trees that filled the air with a heavy green scent. To the left, the empty training buildings showed through the trees, the reflection of our torch occasionally flashing off their sweep of glass windows. To the right, the woods stretched out towards the lake in a maze of bare trunks rising to high flares of evergreen branches. Below their shadows, in the deeper darkness, I could hear the rustle and scraping of night creatures disturbed by our passing. Fir cones crunched underfoot, pressing against the gravel.

"The woods are lovely, dark and deep," I said without thinking about it.

"The woods are bloody noisy," said Jay. "Almost as bad as you."

"Is that a hint that I should just shut up and let you rescue me? Is that what you did, rescue people?"

"No."

"What did you do?"

"Fixed engines, mostly."

"Oh."

"Under fire. Sometimes."

"Oh. Wow. Shutting up now." Though I couldn't help adding, "That's really sexy, you know."

The exasperated noise he made was somehow rather satisfying, but I was good after that. I let him lead me all the way to his door, and as we walked I became less desperate to talk and more aware of every tiny noise and stir of the air around me. Every sound in the undergrowth made me startle, and when we came out into the car park and triggered a security light, it made me flinch. My skin was prickling, and not just because of the cold, and my breathing was coming fast.

I knew, rationally, that it was still the aftermath of fear rushing through me and playing havoc with my nerves. Jay was still holding my hand firmly, however, and he moved me through his door with a sort of quiet certainty that pushed me over an edge I hadn't realized was quite so thin. I definitely wasn't feeling frightened any longer. This was a different type of nervous anticipation.

Jay says I need to stop being so flowery and get to the fucking point. Well, that's exactly where we're headed. To put it bluntly, I was horny as fuck.

Until Jay closed the door behind us and I turned to face him under the bright light in his kitchen, I thought I was the only one. Then I saw the colour splashed across his cheekbones, the brightness of his eyes, the way he was wetting his mouth. Our eyes met for one long slow moment of appraisal.

I'm not sure which of us moved first, but I know I moved faster.

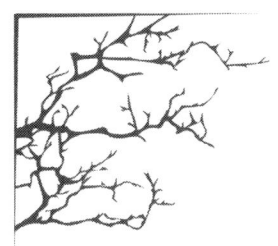

Chapter Seven

I shoved Jay hard against the wall as our mouths crashed together. There was no tenderness in this kiss, only hunger. It was a clumsy clash of lips, teeth, tongue, his hands clawing at my back, my fingers in his hair, clenching around the soft mass of his curls. Our mouths parted for a breath, but then we both dived in again, wet lipped and breathless, his tongue stabbing against mine. Neither of us could pull back long enough to breathe properly, so we gasped against each other, his hand falling down to twist into the waistline of my pyjamas, mine curling open to cup his head and pull him closer.

When he did pull away, I threw my head back to drag in a breath, and he went for my throat, scraping his teeth down the side of my neck to suck sharply at my pulse. I must have let out some noise, because he glanced up, that smirk almost in full flower, and lunged up to take my mouth again.

I wanted more, craved it with every beat of my pulse, wanted skin and heat. I shoved forward again, pressing myself against him, trying to push my thigh between his. He spread his legs for me and then swore into my mouth as he lost his balance slightly. I grabbed his left leg, hooking my hand under his thigh to lift it up, his prosthesis swinging in mid-air.

For a moment, he pulled back, clearly about to protest, but I pushed forward, pressing in so he could ride my leg, his cock a hard ridge under his jeans. Catching his mouth with mine again was instinctive, and after a moment he rose into it, moving against me. I pushed back, rutting against him, and lost myself in his kiss, in the catch and brush of lips, the need and passion of it. I couldn't remember the last time I'd been kissed like this, had never felt like this just from a fully-clothed kiss. Even in my glitter-and-tequila student days, I'd never—

Jay shoved down my pyjama bottoms and gripped my arse, his hands still cold from outside but strong enough to pull me closer. My kiss went loose, and I groped down frantically, trying to get his jeans open without pulling away and only managing to rub him through the denim, moulding my hand over him, trying to get a hint of what lay beneath.

He swore into my mouth again and pushed me back enough to get to his own belt. I took the chance to kick my own bottoms off completely, and then got rid of the sweater and both tops as well. At once my skin prickled at the cold air, but it was worth it for the way Jay stopped to stare, his jeans slipping down his hips as he looked me up and down slowly, his lips parting and his breath coming faster. I drank it in, need pulsing under my skin and beating in my groin. I was getting harder, and it was getting tricky to think past the beat of *now, now, touch me now,* but I knew I liked this. I liked being wanted.

Jay shoved his jeans and boxers farther down, and his cock sprung out, flushed and rigid.

Until then, my only thought had been some vague intention of getting my hand on Jay's cock. Now I had a much better idea. I slid to my knees, curling my hands around his thighs, high enough that I was touching warm skin on each side.

"Luke," Jay breathed, his eyes wide.

I met his gaze, my own breath catching, and for a moment it was more than just sex, more than mere need and lust. He was looking at me as if I was a miracle. I wanted to be that for him, wanted to be something other than the man Danny left behind, the man who waited.

A draft licked under the back door, making the hairs rise on my legs. The floor was hard beneath my knees. Outside, the wind was rising, breathing through the trees with a long sigh.

But Jay was warm under my hands, and I leaned forward to close my mouth over the head of his cock. The moment broke apart, and suddenly it was simply physical, the hint of salt against my tongue, the thick weight of him pushing forward, the quick shudder of his thighs as I sucked him in. It was all movement and heat again, but that sense of more lingered and sank into me until every thrust and shudder rippled through me as well.

When he pushed my head back, I went reluctantly, pulling my mouth off him with a slow slurp.

"Get up here," he ordered, tugging on my shoulders.

I staggered to my feet, not without a surge of dizziness, and he wrapped his arms around me, running his teeth down my ear before he gasped, "Can't balance."

"Bed?"

"Yeah. Fuck."

"Sure," I managed, tipping my head back so he could get to my throat again. "I'm versatile."

He took a shaky breath. "Should have got you naked the first night."

"We didn't like each other then."

"I like you now."

"I noticed." I managed to step back. "Bed. Which way?"

He pointed to the door on the other side of the kitchen, and I backed towards it. He pulled his jeans up enough to walk in them and came after me.

There was a light switch just inside the door that revealed a large room, barely furnished. Jay had a sofa and a telly, and a double bed in the corner with a cheap plastic set of drawers beside it. I threw myself onto the bed, reaching down to give my poor aching cock a quick stroke as he hesitated in the doorway. "I like your bed. Bigger than mine, and it doesn't have any ghosts in it."

He was still staring at me, and it made me crave touch. I forced myself to keep my hand slow, drawing it up and down my cock, and reached up with my other hand to pinch my nipple. Normally I was flustered and guilty in bed, but lying there under his gaze made me feel shameless. I wanted this man to see me.

He turned off the lights.

For a moment, I shuddered. Then, because I'm not daft, I reached out and turned the bedside light on. Jay froze at the end of the bed, his mouth turning down.

"I like it off."

"Tell me where your lube and condoms are, and I'll turn it off when I've found them."

"Er, top drawer. In a tin."

I went rummaging through the drawer and found them. I tossed the condoms at him and helped myself to the lube. I rolled up onto my knees, presenting him with my back, and reached back with my now slick fingers. Touching myself wasn't as good as having him touch me, but I knew how to make this feel good, stroking around the edge of my hole and reaching in just enough to tease and stretch.

"Christ." Jay suddenly moved behind me. I heard his clothes hit the floor, and then the mattress sank behind me. He reached around to close his hand over my cock, and a moment later I felt his lips on the back of my neck. Then he brushed the pad of his thumb against the head of my cock, and I tensed in his arms, my whole body suddenly shaking on the edge.

"Fuck me," I managed. "*Now*, Jay!"

"Hands and knees," he growled in my ear. I pitched forward, hearing the crinkle of foil behind me, and braced my hands against the sheets.

He pressed his cock into me slowly but relentlessly. He was thick enough that the stretch was on that perfect line between pain and delight, but it became pure pleasure when he finally nudged against my prostate. He gave me a moment to adjust, then pulled back, leaving me almost empty. The next thrust was hard and fast, nailing me so perfectly that I clenched my fists in the sheets. He didn't slow down but fucked me fast and fiercely, his breath rasping with each slap of flesh on flesh. It was glorious, and I lifted my hips into every thrust, giving as good as I got, my whole body rising and tightening in readiness.

His hand on my cock was a wonderful shock for all of a moment. Then, just slightly, his knee slipped and he lurched sideways.

It was only a thrust gone awry, his hand sliding off my cock to grab my thigh, but he froze, still balls deep inside me. Then, to my fury, he began to pull out slowly.

"Don't you fucking dare!" I snarled, twisting round to glare at him.

"Might hurt you."

"On your back!"

Jay claimed afterward that I actually grabbed him and put him down against the pillows. Doesn't sound like me, but I can't actually remember. In my defence, I was seconds away from the most spectacular orgasm I'd had in years. So the next I remember, he was spread out below me and I was sinking down to impale myself on his cock.

And it was good.

I rode him hard, and after the first shocked second, he rose into it. His mouth fell open, and he flung his head back, reaching out for me. He locked one hand around my cock, jerking me off clumsily, and I caught his other hand in mine.

Joined like that, I took him. I took the thick swell of his cock lodged inside me, took the widening of his eyes, the sudden groan he let out as his hips snapped up, almost lifting me off the bed, took the way his hands flared open as he shook and came, and then took, as he sank back with hazy eyes, the slow slide of his hand on my cock.

I closed my own hand over his, and it only took two more strokes before I slid over that line too, my release spilling out of me in a long shudder that had my vision turning dark and my whole body sinking down into limp bliss.

I think I might have actually fallen off him. Certainly it was more of a limp roll than a controlled disengagement, and the only thing that stopped me from pitching off the side of the bed was the fact that he rolled with me, putting his arms up to catch me.

We lay there in a tangled heap for a while, just breathing against each other. Then Jay sighed against my shoulder and murmured, "Tell me again. What was the plan for this evening? Stay in your room, watch for the ghost, and don't have sex?"

"One out of three's not that bad." I pulled myself away a little. "Tissues?"

"Box by the sofa."

Well, I was nearer, and he was clearly nowhere near moving yet. I went to get them, and came back to see him spread out over the bed. The lamp had a dim bulb, but it was enough to show him. He was completely slumped against the mattress, eyes half-closed and his whole body relaxed, and I bit back a smile. Not a side of him I'd seen until then.

It also let me see his leg, and I took the opportunity to look as I walked back. It wasn't as bad as I'd feared. His left thigh ended about halfway down. It was covered in what looked like a tight plastic sheath, which connected to the mechanical leg below. That was a mass of gleaming technology, from its articulated knee to the flexible ankle. I'd heard something about the government pledging to fund cutting-edge prosthetics for military amputees, but I'd taken it with a pinch of salt. Our government was good at promises but generally only kept the ones it made to the rich.

Looked like they'd followed through at least once, though.

"Luke?" It was barely more than a mumble, so I dropped a tissue on his stomach.

He grabbed it and mopped at himself half-heartedly. "Come back and sleep."

"About to." A thought occurred to me, and I said cautiously, "Jay, I don't want to step where angels fear to tread or anything, but does your leg still need charging?"

He opened his eyes properly. "Yeah. Crap. Left the charger."

I gulped. "Does that mean one of needs to go and get it?"

"Spare in the kitchen drawer." He was sitting up, and he grabbed for the duvet now, pulling it over his leg.

"I'll get it," I said. "Which drawer?"

"By the kettle."

By the time I got back, his leg was standing by the socket and he was carefully arranged under the duvet, frowning slightly. He still looked sleep-dazed enough to drop at any moment, so I knelt down and plugged the charger in, waving the end at him. "Like a phone charger?"

"Power tool," he said. "Let me."

"I'm right here. Is it too delicate for someone untrained, or are you just uncomfortable?"

He was silent for a while but then said, "Just above the ankle."

He was still sitting up in bed when I rose to my feet again. I hesitated, no longer sure if I was welcome, but he lifted up the corner of the duvet. I dove in, and he reached over me to turn off the light. He curled up against my side again, not quite touching, and said softly, "Full of surprises, you are."

"Because I show some basic consideration?" I moved a little closer. "Hey, Jay?"

"Hmm." He was sinking back towards sleep, and I wondered whether sex always knocked him out like this (for the record, yup, every time).

"Thank you."

"For what?"

"Fucking my brains out."

"Oh, that. My pleasure."

I smiled, pressing my cheek to the pillow, and we slept.

FOR THE SECOND TIME, I woke up with someone's arm flung over my waist. This arm, however, was warm and hairy, with a broad, callused hand that was currently spread possessively over my balls and my increasingly more interested morning wood.

"Jay?" I murmured. "Er, you awake?"

He made a noise against my back that could have been either denial or sleep talking.

I opened my eyes a crack. It was light, and I could see straight out the window and into the woods. There was a deer standing there, gazing across the gravel road with quiet eyes. I could see the frost gleaming on the edge of the ferns, but beyond that the air was dim with mist.

"Oouck?" Jay said, which I interpreted as my name.

"Morning."

He was quiet for a moment, going completely still. Then he said, sounding pleased and bewildered, "You *are* here."

"In the flesh," I said. I rolled my hips slightly, just to remind him of the flesh in question. He closed his hand around me immediately, stroking me lazily. I rocked into it and kept talking. "You saved me from the crazy ghost, remember? My rescuer. Remind me, have I thanked you for that properly yet? I can be very grateful."

"Any more thanks like last night and we'll be dead ourselves before long," he said, but he turned me round gently before reaching for my erection again. His hair was a mess, a whole clump sticking out to the side, and he had a pillow crease across his cheek, but I thought he looked wonderful. He was smiling and his eyes were soft, and I smiled back as I reached down to repay the favour.

"Well, good morning, Luke," he murmured.

"Good morning, Jay," I said brightly, grinning at him. "And how are you this fine morning? Feeling okay?"

"Feeling good," he sighed, eyes falling shut again. He was warm in my hand, and I stroked him gently. I love that perfect softness of the skin stretched over a man's erection, and I relished touching him, watching every tiny stutter of his breath and flush of his cheeks.

"How about this weather? Bit chilly out there, isn't it?"

He opened one eye to glare at me, a little unsuccessfully. "Luke."

"Bit of a nip in the air." I leaned forward enough to catch his lower lip between my teeth.

"Puns?" he said, but his breathing roughened. "At this hour?"

"It's morning."

"Should be banned until dinnertime."

I grinned at him, running my free hand up to play with his nipples and stroke through his chest hair. "You'll have to find a better use for my mouth."

"Will I?" he said and moved quickly. Within a moment I was flat on my back and he was kissing me deeply. I writhed against him happily, and he only kissed me harder, his hand still warm and steady on my cock.

It was a while before we stumbled out of bed, and I was a little disappointed that he made us take separate showers, although I was pretty certain it was just because he didn't want me seeing the leg he'd managed to keep beneath the sheets throughout our morning entertainment. I ventured into the kitchen to find my pj's and started coffee while I was there. It was a nice way to begin the day, and I enjoyed it. It was these things that I missed, the little things.

Jay came in a few minutes later, his hair flat from the shower and his jeans and leg back on. He gave me an approving nod. "Spare clothes in the bathroom. Across the hall."

I stole a kiss from him before I went.

He was frying bacon and tomatoes and scrambling eggs when I got back, and I sat myself down with coffee. "When are you working today?"

"Day off." He gave me a sideways look. "New Year's Eve."

"Is it?" I asked, genuinely startled. "Time flies."

"You got plans?"

I'd said maybe to a workmate's party, but had never been keen. "Nothing I can't cancel. You?"

"This afternoon, yeah." He looked at me thoughtfully. "Come with?"

"To what?"

He just chuckled. "Wait and see."

"I was going to go back to the library."

He swung to glare at me. "No. Tell them to send someone else."

"Military historians don't just grow on trees, you know, and I need the money. Besides, I think she wants my help."

"Nice way she has of asking."

I shrugged. "I've never heard that communicating with the dead is easy. The bacon's burning."

He swore and turned back to the stove. "Don't want you to get hurt."

"I'll be careful."

"Right."

The toaster sprung up at that point, so I went to collect the toast. Jay poured tomato and bacon onto plates at the same moment and then added the eggs in a buttery heap, impressing me. I could never get all the bits of a proper cooked breakfast hot at the same time. He put a plate down in my place, plucked a piece of toast from my fingertips, and said, "You'll sleep here from now on. Not in that house."

"You think we're safe from her here?"

He shrugged. "Built in the seventies. Reckon she's older than that."

"Do you think that makes a difference? I don't really know how ghosts work. It's not like there's been much reputable scientific study of them. If the story is right, even the chest was imported from Italy."

"You should really move to a hotel."

"Money," I reminded him, drawing the word out. "Besides, I am not staying in the centre of bloody Aldershot on New Year's Eve."

He considered that. "Fair point."

"So," I said, relaxing. "Where are you taking me today?"

Jay smiled. "To the races."

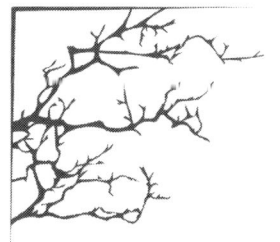

Chapter Eight

He took me stock car racing. I'm not even going to attempt to recall or explain what we watched, because ten years on I still don't understand it half the time, and I've seen a lot more now. Suffice to say it involved lots of cars, of what seemed like varying levels of suitability for the task, being driven very fast around a small track and occasionally spinning off it in spectacular ways.

Sorry, love, I'm still not a car person.

Despite having no idea what was going on, I started enjoying myself within minutes, not so much because of the on-track mayhem (no, ssh, you, I know it's all meticulously organized, but even you can't deny it looks like mayhem to a novice), but because of the crowds. Everyone seemed to be very jolly and very loud, in the way men are when given free rein to enthuse about the machines they love—and the crowd was mostly, but not entirely, male. Jay was obviously well-known here, and he was greeted by cheerful shouts and insults.

I got a few puzzled looks, but Jay just shrugged and kept saying, "Luke. He's with me."

That seemed to be enough, though one or two threw out curious remarks. One, who had introduced himself as Fat Gary, said casually, "Mostly bangers today. That your thing?"

Jay had vanished under a car by then, so I just said, "I know nothing about any of this. Look good fun, though."

"Yeah? Mate of Jay's?" He sounded a bit dubious.

"Military historian. Working at Eelmoor Hall." I was aware a couple of the others were listening, so I added lightly, "I'm completely ignorant about cars, but you want to know anything about the British Army before World War I, I'm your man."

"Yeah?" Fat Gary said, sounding amused. "Well, if I ever need to phone a friend...."

"So," one of the younger lads mentioned, edging nearer, "I heard they used to put stuff in the food to, y'know, make it hard to stand to attention." He made a drooping movement with his hand. "Bit of sedating the trouser snake, if you know what I mean."

Seriously, you have no idea how often I get asked about that one.

"Saltpetre," I said cheerfully. "Soldiers have been claiming that since the Battle of Waterloo. Sorry—all lies, or at least unproven. And given how the birth-rate goes up during every war, if they did try it, it didn't work very well. Mind you, I once interviewed a chap who landed on the beaches on D-day. He swore blind they'd been spiking his food all the way through the war. Only thing was, he reckoned it hadn't actually kicked in until he turned seventy."

It got me a round of groans and a slap on the back, and that seemed to be enough for most of them. Jay had reappeared briefly, looking grease stained and happy, but had been dragged off again quickly. Fat Gary took me under his wing, patiently trying to explain all the different classes of car and the reasons for the various bits of gear. I didn't understand a word of it, but I enjoyed myself anyway. The noise and the camaraderie, the cold bright sky and the warm buzz of a greasy hot dog for lunch, all came together to lift my spirits. Life was good, and it got a little better when Jay reappeared beside me, his hat pulled down low over his curls and his face bright with pleasure.

I forgot the ghost completely until we were driving home and Jay said, "Last chance to get a hotel room."

"Nice thought, but no. I want to get back to work tomorrow. I'm going to try and research her properly, too. That way, either I finish the job as fast as possible and get the hell out once I'm done, or I deal with her directly."

"I don't like it."

"No disrespect, but you don't have to like it. It's my call." *What if it was Danny*, I was still thinking. *What if he needed me to find him, and this was the only way he could get me to listen? Things are only missing until they're found again.*

"She's still in the box," I said out loud.

Jay didn't take his eyes off the road, though I saw his hands tighten on the wheel. It was twilight, the day fading into brown and silver shadows, the sort of hour when foxes came dashing across the road out of the woods or herons went flashing low over the rust-brown ferns, heading home to the green quiet of the canal. I could already see Eelmoor Hall looming ahead of us, set on its hillside. The windows were dark.

"How'd you get that?" Jay asked, turning off the main road.

"Last night." I quoted, not without a shiver, "It's so cold in this box."

"Could mean her grave. You said she'd been found."

"It's a legend. The edges have been smoothed off. Take it back to basics, and we've just got a story about a girl going missing on her wedding night. We've also got a story about a girl who died locked inside a chest. Maybe the same girl, maybe two or four or even ten different girls. Stories accumulate details over the years. They merge and split and get dramatic details added on. Hell, weren't you ever warned not to lock yourself in a cupboard when you were playing hide-and-seek?"

"Yeah. So, what, you think our girl's still in there? How'd we get the legend here?"

"A ghostly bride, a famous story, and maybe I'm not the only one she's spoken to. 'It's so cold in this box,' she said. If she's said it to people before, the story could even have started here and then got confused with other versions over the years."

"You seriously think this is a possibility?"

I considered it as we slowed towards the hall's gates. "I'm not sure I could be happy with myself if I didn't give it serious thought." They'd searched a lot of places after Danny vanished, storm drains and derelict houses, places where someone might get trapped. They hadn't found him, not even with dogs, but I imagined the Bride's husband. How well had he known her? Was she his sweetheart or had it been an arranged match? Had he been nervous, looking at this girl he was supposed to bed for the first time that night, expected to love and protect? When had he realized that the game, that silly, flirtatious game, had gone wrong?

"What's it like, this chest?" Jay asked.

"Long lost, though there's a replica in the library." I considered that. "Which suggests she *was* found. How else would they know what it looked like?"

"Damn." The gates swung open, and we started up the drive. Shivers were beginning to crawl up my spine again, but I was managing to ignore them until Jay asked, "Is it open?"

"What?"

"The one in the library."

"No." I looked at him as our lights cut through the dusk. "Shit. No way. Not out in plain sight like that."

"No." He didn't sound sure, though, and after a moment I realized we hadn't turned off to the staff quarters but were driving up towards the main entrance.

"You want to look now?"

"You want to sleep with that hanging over us?"

I shuddered. "You had to go and say it, didn't you?"

"Regretting that."

He took us round the side of the house to the north face, where there was a bay originally designed for coaches.

"I'm just going to look quickly. Stay here."

"Like hell."

He glared at me. "Luke. Stay in the car."

"You're not going in there alone. Not after dark."

"She's not after *me*."

"We'll be fine as long as we keep the lights on. I'll do star jumps in front of the sensors if I have to, but I am not sitting here while you go and look for bodies by yourself!"

"Bodies? Only looking for one."

So we both went into the library. We entered the house through a door I hadn't even tried yet. It opened into the grand foyer at the north end of the building, from which we could access the east corridor and the library foyer. The lights came on as soon as we stepped in, and Jay left me pacing up and down the marbled floor, peering into the dark doorways around us. He unlocked a cupboard while I stared up at the sweep of the staircase and the paintings that looked down on us from the shadows. It was very dark upstairs. Eelmoor's treasures would be sold with the house, and I wondered why the army had left it in the care of just one man.

"Why hasn't this place been burgled?"

"The good stuff is all locked away in storage somewhere. These are just old family pictures, and they all have alarms."

I laughed, darting another glance at the darkness upstairs. "Family pictures. I just have a Facebook album and some dodgy photos of eighties weddings. What have you got—whoa!"

Jay hefted the very large crowbar he had just pulled out of the cupboard. "Might need it."

We went through to the library, and I led Jay into the museum. I moved Winston the mouldy bulldog aside gently, and we both looked down at the chest. It was big, studded with metal, and solidly made. The wood was dark. It looked like something a pirate would own.

"Wouldn't get either of us in there," Jay commented.

"No." I imagined my sister Katie, who was shorter and slighter than me. She'd fit, and the thought made me shiver and wave sharply at the sensors just to be safe. "A smallish woman would have space to spare, though."

He put the crowbar down. "Let's try lifting the lid first."

We had to heave, one on each corner, but it came up in a plume of dust.

The only things in the chest were a few dead moths, a pile of neatly folded old newspapers, and a faded photo of a young Prince Charles shaking someone's hand on the terrace.

Jay rocked back on his heels, letting out a gasp of relieved laughter. Then he threw his arm around my waist and said, "Okay. Let's go and see the new year in."

"Got a wild party planned?" I asked, leaning on him.

"I was thinking Jools Holland on the telly, glass of something posh and fizzy at midnight, and a shag."

"Sounds like my kind of new year."

"Got the keys to the observatory. Could watch the fireworks from there."

"There's an observatory? Yeah, sure. Can we take the champagne with us?" I waggled my eyebrows at him. "Maybe the shag as well."

"Steep staircase," he said. "Get me drunk up there, I'm not coming down until morning. And nope, not enough space to lie down."

"Shame," I said, turning round enough that we were pressed together. I was just leaning in when the boards in the gallery creaked softly.

"Time to go," Jay said.

Out in the foyer, I looked at the stairs. "We should probably get what we left in my room."

"Luke. It's not—"

"I want my phone and laptop, and some clean undies, and your charger. She's never hurt me while I'm awake."

He shook his head hard, but I was a little bit angry now. She had no right to scare us away from our own belongings or interfere with my work. Shrugging Jay off, I dashed up the stairs.

It took a moment to get orientated at the top, but I soon found my way through to the residential corridor, waving my arms above my head to be certain the sensors would stay on. Our stuff was where we'd left it, and I hurled all my belongings into my bag at random and then tucked Jay's charger in the top. I admit to scurrying a little as I headed back for the stairs, but nothing happened. No footsteps or soft sighs or messages whispered against my neck.

When I got back, I found Jay halfway up the stairs staring up at the wall. He'd obviously started after me, and I slunk back down sheepishly, expecting to be growled at.

But something else had caught his attention, and when I reached him, he just said, "Look. The picture."

I followed his pointing hand. The wall was one of those grand galleries where every space was filled with portraits—a montage of formal poses, stiff hats, and limp ringlets. The picture Jay was pointing at was of a young woman. Her dress looked Jacobean, maybe a little later, to me: white silk and silver tissue, every seam picked out with bows or frills of lace. She held an armful of greenery, fir boughs, and the pearly gleam of mistletoe. A paler woman might have looked insipid in it, but it suited her. She was dark haired, dark eyed, and lovely, and there was trouble in her smile for all she looked barely more than a girl. She had the kind of face you'd see plastered across an advertising board today, probably in connection with very expensive perfume, designer underwear, or absurdly priced handbags.

"There she is," Jay said. And then, at my puzzled glance, "Look at the plaque."

Ginevra Treggio, 1641, it read. Underneath it, though, was another, more Victorian in style. This one said, *The Mistletoe Bride.*

"Ginevra," I said, and the quality of the silence changed around us, suddenly watchful.

"Definitely time to go," Jay said and dragged me back out to the car.

BACK AT HIS, I WAS already reaching for my laptop when he cleared his throat and said, "New Year's Eve."

Oh, right. Telly, followed by champagne, fireworks, and shagging.

He'd got the telly on by the time I'd made up my mind to resist all research-related temptation. He was already sprawled out on the sofa, and he lifted his arm slightly. I dropped beside him with a sense of wonder, pressing up against his side.

You know what you don't get from ten years of occasional one-night stands? You don't get to snuggle on the sofa in front of mindless telly. It felt strange at first, something I couldn't quite remember how to do. How did I fit my shoulder and elbow in? Was I going to spoil the moment if I dropped my hand onto his thigh, and where was I supposed to put it otherwise?

"Luke," Jay said, kissing the top of my head. "Relax."

"I'm trying."

He grunted sceptically and then moved me. I wasn't averse to being man-handled a little, so I went with it, letting him pull me over his lap until I was leaning back against his chest, our legs stretched out and his arms around me. "Better?"

It was. I pressed my cheek to his chest and vaguely tried to watch the telly, revelling in the strange luxury of this. I was a little afraid of it, scared that guilt would suddenly close around me. It didn't feel like I was betraying Danny, though, didn't feel like something he would hate me for. It just felt good.

I can't remember exactly what we were watching. It was some comedy review of the year, something that made Jay laugh occasionally, every chuckle rumbling against me. After a while, he began to rub my belly. It was so soft and slow I wasn't sure he even knew he was doing it, but it did more to relax me than anything else.

"Thank you," I said.

"For what?" He glanced down at me and smiled.

"It was a good day."

"Yeah. It was." He leaned down and kissed me, slow and easy, not demanding anything, just a slow, warm press of lips to lips. "It really was."

He slid his hand under my T-shirt and went back to rubbing my belly. I arched back against him with a happy mumble, and he laughed again. "Part cat, are you?"

"No, but don't let that stop you."

He kissed the side of my throat—once, twice, again—and then slid my belt undone and thumbed the top button of my jeans open.

"Let me turn round so I can reach you." I sat up a little.

He kissed my cheek and pulled me down again. "No. Just take this one."

"That's not—"

"Luke. *Relax.*" He got the rest of my buttons undone and reached in to close his hand around my rapidly filling cock.

I stopped protesting, sinking back against him. He leaned down to kiss me again, and I gave myself up to it, throwing my arm around his neck and lifting my hips into his touch. He had good hands, callused but sure, steadily working me towards melting point, and I forgot to worry, forgot to second-guess him, forgot to make sure that he was too satisfied to leave me, and just let him touch me. I felt so warm, as if I was filled from head to toe with heat, not blazing and hungry but softly overwhelming.

When I came, it rose through me in a hot surge and I spilled into Jay's hand. He kissed me through every shudder and gasp and then hung onto me when I went so limp I nearly slid right off the sofa. When I opened my eyes, he was looking smug and delighted.

"You're fun to play with," he commented.

"I'll show you fun," I threatened rather vaguely. I made an actual effort to slide onto the floor then, landing in front of him. From here the bulge in his jeans was very apparent, so I leaned in to rub my cheek against it. "Nice. Lift your hips."

"Don't always have to reciprocate," he pointed out, but he was already busy undoing his jeans and lifting himself up. I tugged them down to his knees, smirking when I saw how his cock was already pushing out of his boxers towards me. I reached out to push his knees apart, wetting my lips. My left hand hit warm flesh, but my right hand landed on smooth plastic.

Jay froze. Then he jerked his jeans up hard on that side, knocking my hand away as he tried to cover his thigh.

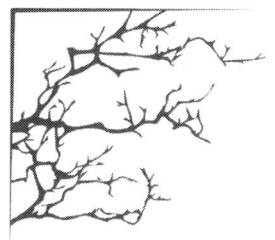

Chapter Nine

"I'm not going to judge," I said, looking up at him.

"I don't want you to see."

"You've seen my damage," I reminded him. The delighted smile had faded, and he looked grim again. I was beginning to learn how to read his face, though, and I was pretty sure that scowl meant unhappiness, not hostility.

"Not the same thing. You're not broken."

"Nor are you."

He snorted, pulling himself back to sit up straight. "Missing a few vital parts here."

"That's not the same as broken," I told him and pulled myself up to sit beside him. I took his hand, though he clenched it under my palm. "Jay. Look, I don't know if you want to hear this, or even if it will help you, but I'm a few years further down the same road. I know what it feels like to have your whole world suddenly break apart around you. I might not have the physical scars, but I get it. I do. And yeah, this is what I learned along the way. I don't think it's the things that happen to us that decide whether we're broken. I think it's how we choose to live with the things we can't control."

He was looking at me now, his eyes wide.

"And I was broken," I continued. "It took a lot of people and a lot of time before I wasn't. I'm still mending, but—"

He lifted his hand and pressed his finger to my lips, silencing me. Then he ran his hand up to brush the faintly crooked line of my nose and the slash across my eyebrow. "You do have scars."

I blinked at him. "I forgot. I don't notice them much anymore."

"You're not broken." He said it testingly, rather than as a statement of fact, then nodded. "Okay."

"You live your life," I said. "Today—the friends you have, the enjoyment you took in, y'know, engines and stuff, all that. You couldn't do that if you were broken."

"Engines and stuff?" he echoed with a grimace. "Did you not pay any attention?"

"Not a car person," I reminded him. "I mean, it was fun, and I liked the little three-wheelers, but I have no idea what was—"

He kissed me. I assumed it was to shut me up, but he lingered, turning it tender, and when he drew back his eyes were bright. "Thank you."

To my surprise, he stood up, pulling his jeans back up.

"Jay?" I said. "I still owe you—"

He held out his hand. "Lost the mood. Sorry."

"Not your fault," I said, taking his hand and pulling myself up. It still made me feel a little off-balance, though. "I'll catch up later."

"It's sex. Not tit for tat."

I shrugged.

"Luke." He was frowning at me a little. "No one's keeping count."

Sex had been something it was easy to give Danny. I'd always counted, as if I could trade extra orgasms for hours when he'd stay in the safety of our bed. It hadn't always worked, but he'd never looked elsewhere for sex. That had been something to cling to in the eye of the storm, when the man I'd loved was vanishing into his own pain and addiction.

Jay's hand on my cheek brought me back to the present.

"Food?" he said.

I let the past slide away. "Sure. What culinary wonders did you have in mind?"

He headed into the kitchen. "Would you complain if I didn't do anything fancy? Cheese on toast?"

"You know, that might be exactly what I fancy." I was surprised by how suddenly it appealed, with a sudden flush of hunger. "You got any ketchup?"

He smiled back at me. "Course."

We must have gone through most of a loaf, loading the grill up with more after every serving. Hot cheese, toast crisp on the edges and melting soft in the middle, the tang of ketchup; I can still taste it if I concentrate, still remember the comfort of it. I've dined in medieval halls and posh London restaurants, even eaten in the Officer's Mess at Sandhurst, but that simple meal, in the shab-by warmth of the kitchen in the staff quarters at Eelmoor Hall that New Year's Eve, was one of the best I've ever had. We ate it sitting at the kitchen table, elbows knocking, taking turns trying to pinch the ketchup from each other, laughing.

When I was too full to eat any more, I sat back and licked the last grease off my fingers. "Wow. I don't think I can move now. Bring me a pillow. I'll sleep right here tonight."

"You'll sleep with me tonight," Jay said. I turned to smile at him, and he added, "You've got crumbs."

"Where?"

He touched the corner of my mouth. "There." Then he kissed them off.

(Mark's here this afternoon, and he's just leaned over my shoulder and made gagging noises. Piss off, mate. This is my happy memory, and I'll wallow if I want to.

Odd, that. I hadn't really anticipated writing about happy things in this ac-count.

Anyway, Ciara's yelling at me to stop being an antisocial git and go help Jay with the barbecue, so I'll be back in a bit, dear reader.)

WE WERE STILL IN THE kitchen when Jay glanced at the clock and said, "If you want to see the fireworks, we should start walking."

I wasn't too bothered about them, not when the alternative was to stay here and keep exchanging crumbly, ketchup-flavoured kisses instead, but he'd men-tioned them twice now. I leaned back and said, "You want to."

"Missed it last year." He added, before I could prompt him, "I wasn't good with the noise then."

"Better now, though?"

"Yeah."

"Okay, then. Let me find my coat."

Suitably fortified against the cold, we headed outside. Jay pointed his torch ahead of us, but there was no other light save the narrow moon. The night was hushed, with only the sigh of the wind through the trees to muffle our footsteps, and neither of us spoke.

Jay led us away from the house, up the hillside. The main hall was a little way down the slope, where it could command a view but be spared the full lash of the north wind, but he led me past it. The path led uphill, zigzagging or leading up short flights of steps in places. I was beginning to adjust to Jay's pace by then—on the flat, he could go at a natural pace, slopes were slower, and steps were difficult but not impossible. I'd jogged up here a few mornings ago, though I hadn't noticed any observatory, and I was a little sobered to realize how much I took it for granted that I could move at speed when I wanted to.

He hadn't been okay with the noise of the fireworks last year. He'd mentioned an IED, that first day. It had been long enough for his hair to grow out, but I wasn't sure if that told me anything useful. British soldiers didn't sport buzzcuts, so Jay's curls could have grown past his collar in a few months. Before I thought about it, I asked aloud, "How long ago?"

He didn't need to ask what I meant. "Fifteen months, give or take."

I didn't make the mistake of saying sorry again, but I reached out and caught his hand, squeezing it lightly. He gripped it back for a moment and then asked, with a note of amusement, "Are those mittens?"

"I keep telling you. I get cold."

He squeezed my hand hard and then let go. "Up here."

He swung his torch around. I'd seen the building in front of us on my run, but I'd assumed it was a folly or a particularly elaborate potting shed. I'd been expecting a tower with a domed roof, but this was one story high, perched on the summit of the hill. If it had ever had a dome, it had long vanished. It had a metal-covered door, padlocked shut.

Jay passed me the torch and unlocked the door. He then held it open with a flourish. I entered warily, swinging the torch around. I was pleasantly surprised. The walls were plastered stone and lined with cupboards. In one corner, sure enough, there was a stack of flowerpots and an old lawnmower, but the rest was neat. A little metal spiral staircase led up one side towards a hatch in the roof.

"That's on a latch," Jay said, waving towards it. "Easier for you."

I scrambled up the steps to push it open, gasping as the cold wind rushed over me. I climbed out and turned the torch back onto the stairs for Jay. As I waited for him to lever himself up, I looked around and breathed in sharply as I took in the view. Even in the darkness of the night, I could see for miles.

To the south and east, the lights of Aldershot rose in long sweeps over the dark hillsides. I could see where the ridges must stand, not by the shapes they made against the sky, but by the few tiny lights moving along them in bright ribbons, cars on the high roads. Behind us, on the other side of the canal, Farnborough's small airport stretched out in long lines, illuminated even on a night with no flights, with the town behind it. On the other sides, the hills rose up, speckled with patches of lights where clusters of houses or small villages perched among the soft folds of the downs. On a moonless light, the ground was hidden, and the night seemed to be full of veils of floating lights.

"Funny," Jay said. "Don't realize, when you're here on your own, how close to civilization we are."

"It's beautiful."

"It is." He took a slow breath of his own. "It really is."

In the distance, a mile away, church bells began to chime the hour. Before they were half done, the first rockets went squealing up. Jay tensed a little beside me, and I reached for his hand.

And light flowered across the sky, boom after boom heralding pink and silver shimmers, globes of blue and green stars, scarlet flashes, more and more and more, until the faint scent of cordite came softly to us on the wind. As each round of fireworks faded, little flickering sparks kept floating onwards, paper lanterns drifting across the sky.

Start the year how you mean to go on, they say. I started it hand in hand with Jay, gazing up at the sky in wonder.

It's funny, because whenever someone mentions that winter to me, I think of the ghost first, but that was a good new year. I should remember that more often.

We walked back across the gardens quietly. There were still occasional fireworks going off in the distance, though we were a good half hour into 2015 by then.

"Won't get any sleep for a while," Jay commented.

"Gosh, whatever could we do to pass the time? Hand of bridge? Quick game of Monopoly?"

"Promised you champagne, fireworks, and shagging."

"Have you actually got champagne?" I demanded, waking up a little.

"Yup. Well, fizzy wine, at least. Boss gives us all a bottle for Christmas."

"Generous man."

"Only five of us. Hard stuff to drink on your own, though."

I tucked my arm through his. "Aren't you lucky I'm here to help."

"More your style than mine."

I glanced up at him. Had that been a little bit of wariness in his voice? "I'm not actually that posh, you know."

"Sound it."

"Acquired it along the way. We're middle class, my family. I just picked up the accent and enough mannerisms to pass after I went up to Oxford. Useful camouflage. It still opens some doors, especially with retired officers. Closes others."

He shook his head a little but didn't say anything. He didn't pull away from me either, so I took that as a win. Back in his kitchen, he got the wine out of the fridge and dug through the cupboards for a couple of wine glasses. When we lifted our glasses, Jay tapped his against mine lightly. "Happy New Year, Luke."

"Happy New Year," I murmured back. "Cheers."

Fizzy wine makes me giddy and giggly every time. It's not something I'm proud of, but I can't switch it off, either. By Jay's crooked smile, he found it very entertaining by the time, two glasses later, that he scooped me from the kitchen to his bed.

"Lightweight."

"I'm really not," I protested, discarding my clothes in a trail behind me. "I just have a terrible weakness for—*oh*!" I descended into laughter again as he lifted his mouth from my shoulder, where he had just pressed a quick kiss.

"Ticklish?"

"Not usually."

He tumbled me down onto the bed, and I held up my arms up for him. He smiled down at me and said, "Wait."

And as I watched, wine and laughter still bubbling through me, he undressed for me. The sweater and T-shirt went first, but then, to my amazement, he bent down to take off his shoes and then pushed his jeans down.

I sat up, waiting for him to tell me to look away, but he didn't. He kept his eyes on me but carefully shook his jeans off before he pushed his boxers down after them.

He wasn't hard, but I understood. I could see the way his shoulders were braced, the clench of every muscle in his thighs, the wariness in his eyes. He swallowed hard, lifting his chin, and said, "There. You can look."

I did, taking my time to be sure he noticed. He was all tense strength, his arms straight at his side, his stomach rigid, his shoulders out, and his gaze straight forward. His left thigh vanished into the sleek sheath of his prosthesis, but his upper body was all solid muscle, the sort I was far too lazy to ever work for in the gym. There were other scars scattered across his torso, cutting palely across the pelt of fair hair that covered his chest and arrowed down his abdomen, but nothing else as discordant as the sleek artificiality of his leg. Put all together, though, the story his body told was one of power and endurance.

"Bloody gorgeous," I said and tried to put all my appreciation into my voice.

His eyes darted down, and I suddenly realized that he wasn't just standing on display. He was standing to attention.

Look, in my defence, I'd never seen anyone do it out of uniform before, let alone stark naked.

As soon as I realized, I knelt up and threw my arms around his neck, pressing my cheek to his and repeating, "Gorgeous. Absolutely gorgeous."

He grabbed my hand, hard enough that it hurt, and dragged it down, pressing my hand against his prosthesis. "Even that?"

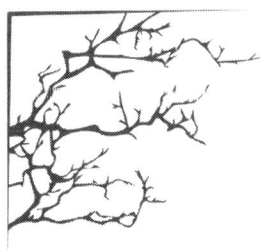

Chapter Ten

I tried to think past the last of the fizz to pick the right words. I'd been good at this once, had learned the necessity of tiptoeing my way across Danny's mental minefield. It took me a moment, though, before I managed to say, very carefully, "By itself, no. As part of the whole? I *really* like the whole package. A replacement part isn't going to scare me off."

Jay pulled back sharply, staring at me. "Expected a polite lie."

"You know," I said, leaning in as I spoke, "I haven't known you very long, but I'm pretty sure you wouldn't appreciate lies."

"Nope." He met my kiss, and I felt him melt out of his stiff posture, his body pressing warmly against mine. After a moment, he moved, settling beside me on the bed. He pulled away, holding me back a little, and said quietly, "Leg needs charging."

"I'll turn my back."

He caught my wrist. "It's okay."

I sat back, watching as he reached down to his leg. He got as far as leaning down to switch it off, and then hesitated. For a moment we both sat there, staring at his leg. Then he dropped his head and said, "Luke. I—"

Kissing his shoulder lightly, I reminded him, "You have nothing to prove."

I lay with my eyes closed for a few minutes, listening to him move around. When the bedside light went dark, I opened my eyes. He was sitting on the side of the bed again, and when I reached out, I found that his back was bowed. I could see the little blink of his leg charging, but that was nowhere near enough light to see his expression.

I ran my hand up and down his back, and slowly he relaxed and began to sit up. Emboldened, I sat up and lifted his hair off his nape so I could kiss him there.

"That's nice," he sighed, his shoulders relaxing a little, so I did it again and then went on to scatter kisses across his back and shoulders, keeping it light and tender. The fireworks had finally stopped, and it was very quiet in there, as if we were the only people left in the world. When he turned his head and sought my mouth, I kissed him back hard. He twisted around, his arms coming up around me, pushing me back, and perhaps inevitably, I lost my balance. We went tumbling down against the pillows, mouths locked together. It wasn't as urgent as the night before, but it still lit me up, and I ran my hands across every bit of him I could reach, wrapped my legs around his, and kept kissing, our mouths meeting and parting breathlessly in the dark.

I rubbed my foot against his right calf, needing to touch him in as many places as possible, and shifted my other leg, instinctively trying to do the same on both sides. There was nothing there, of course, but the movement pressed our thighs together, and I felt where his ended—a cold space where warm flesh should have been.

He tensed a little, pulling his mouth back, but I couldn't let him. He felt too good against me, warmth and strength and the hard rub of his erection against mine. I ran my hand down his back again, letting it slide gently over the sweat that slicked him, and cupped his bum, squeezing deliberately.

"Nice arse," I said and made it as leering as I could.

He snorted but then murmured, "Say the sweetest things, you do."

And all my champagne giggles came rushing back. I tried to hold them back, but they rolled up through me anyway, and I dissolved. Jay started to laugh as well.

It's hard to kiss someone when you're both laughing. Hard, but wonderful. Suddenly, all the awkwardness was, well, not gone, but irrelevant, and we went tumbling over the bed together, hands and mouths busy. He nipped my shoulder. I licked his ear. He tickled me, and I squirmed and wriggled, laughing into the side of his neck, finding his armpit, where I lavished a kiss that made him jump. I wriggled round so I could blow raspberries against his flat belly, and then caught the end of his cock in my mouth as it bounced damply against my cheek, sucking lightly as he groaned.

He kissed the back of my knee, where I'd lodged it against the pillows, and then pushed my thighs apart. He sucked my balls lightly, and I sighed around his cock as sparks shot through me. I shifted enough that I could lean in and fit as much of him as possible into my mouth, and he gasped against the base of my cock.

When he began to brush kisses up my length, I closed my eyes and let everything else go. This was the only moment that mattered, this easy, unrushed exchange of pleasure. There was none of the urgency of the night before, just the slow, warm ripple of delight moving back and forth between us. In the darkness there was nothing to see, but I could feel everything—every brush of his tongue and tightening of his lips, every damp trickle of spit, and the hot, soft wetness of the inside of his cheek pressing against the head of my cock. He was hard as steel in my mouth, jerking forward slightly every time I ran my tongue over his slit. I could smell him, a hint of musk tangled with the damp salt of sweat and spit, and it just turned me on more. I was shivering from head to foot, so alert that every sensation became pleasure, from the rough press of his stubbled cheek against my inner thigh, to the ache in my jaw, to the gathering heat in my balls.

I tried to make it last, wanted to float forever in this cloud of delight, but I felt the moment when it became too much for Jay, when he suddenly began to push his hips forward, when he groaned around me, his mouth suddenly urgent. It tipped me over into pure need, and I went at him like I'd never get to suck cock again, my whole body suddenly reduced to two points of glorious sensation.

He pulled off me with a cry, hips arching up, his cock stiffening further for one moment before he came in a spurt of hot salt. He shook and shuddered with it, and I kept my mouth on him even as I lost control of the rest of my body, shoving my cock forward into the air in a blind hope for touch.

To my immense relief, he had his hand on me again in seconds, stroking hard and fast. Then his mouth descended again, a little slack and lazy but enough, more than enough, because I was coming, all that delight gathering and bursting out of me as I dropped my head onto his thigh and groaned.

Neither of us moved for a while.

I was beginning to wonder if he was asleep when he reached down and ran his hand through my hair. "Luke."

"Is that my name?" I managed. "I've forgotten. Fucking *hell*, Jay."

He laughed. "Yeah."

We lay and breathed for a bit longer. Then he said, "Er, Luke?"

"Mmm?"

"You're lying on my leg."

I was pretty much lying on all of him at that point, so it took me a moment to get what he meant. Then I realized that I'd dropped my head onto his left thigh. I sat up in a hurry. "Shit, was I hurting you?"

He was quiet for a moment. "No. No, you were fine. Just not sure you noticed."

"I didn't," I said. "I was so comfortable. I'll move."

"Don't have to." He took a slow breath. "Liked it."

I found myself swallowing hard. Carefully, I lay down again, pillowing my face back onto his leg. Before I could think better of it, I dropped a kiss onto the soft skin of his inner thigh.

"Actually, no," he said, voice rough. "Get up here."

"I'm sorry," I said, but he pulled me in hard, hugging me so tightly that I could barely breathe. Even when he relaxed that grip, he held me close, pressing his face against my shoulder and mumbling something.

"What?" I asked.

"I said you're one of the good ones, aren't you?"

I had to swallow again. By the time I'd found the words to reply, his breathing had slowed enough that I knew he was asleep. I still whispered, "So are you, Jay," but I don't think he heard me. Not that time.

I WOKE UP FIRST AND couldn't quite manage to snuggle peacefully. My mind was too full, and I eventually left Jay to sleep and went through to the kitchen. It was early, not quite light, and very quiet. Trying not to wake Jay, I tiptoed through making coffee and set my laptop up on the table.

I had a name and a date. With that, any half-competent researcher should be able to find out exactly who our ghost had been.

It took me fifteen minutes and multiple variations on her name, and trying to piece sense out of a translated web page from a local-studies library in Genoa, but from that I tracked down her husband's name, and from there it all fell into place very quickly.

By the time Jay came in, dressed and bleary-eyed, I had pieced it all together and was sitting back to sip my coffee.

"Morning," he grunted and looked around before adding forlornly, "Coffee?"

I got him a cup, and he slid into the chair next to me, squinting at my laptop. "Up early."

"I found her," I said. "Well, her story, at least."

"Yeah?" He took the coffee and pulled me down for a quick toothpaste-flavoured kiss. "Hi."

"Hi, yourself," I said and probably grinned stupidly with it. I'd forgotten how to do this whole shared-morning thing. "You working today?"

"After lunch. What's the story?"

"It's sad," I told him. "Breakfast?"

"Don't fancy much. You okay with toast?"

"I'm good," I said and pushed him back down into his chair. "I'll do it. I'm awake."

As I filled the toaster, I told him what I'd found. "She *was* Italian."

"Box is meant to be, right?"

"Yeah, but I think that's a later invention. Maybe a garbled version of the real story. She was definitely here before she died. She married the younger son of Sir Walter Tichborne, who was the one who commissioned the house in 1617."

"Been here all along?"

"I think so."

"How did an Italian girl marry a Hampshire lad? There's jam in the fridge and Marmite in that cupboard. Have whichever, but pass the Marmite, please."

I got them out, discovering an actual toast rack in the cupboard in the process. "It's a little vague, but I think her father was part of the Genoese delegation in London. They were minor nobility over there. I found a line about her being a renowned beauty at court, and Sir Walter was the local MP at that time. There's plenty of ways she could have met young Antony."

"That was his name?"

"Yeah. Antony Tichborne. They would have had religion in common, at least, him being a Tichborne."

"Supposed to mean something to me?"

I shook my head. "Only if you're a history geek. Our Tichbornes were a cadet branch of a very old family, Winchester way. I think there are still descendants there, but the important thing about them in this period was that they were known for being very strongly Catholic even in times when that was po-tentially lethal. Antony's sister went to the continent and took up holy orders, for instance. There was even a cousin who got caught up in the Babington Plot a few generations earlier and got hung, drawn, and quartered for it."

"Assume I know nothing about history."

"Plot to assassinate Elizabeth I and replace her with her Catholic cousin, Mary, Queen of Scots. Chidiock Tichborne was his name. He wrote a poem the night before his execution. They call it 'Tichborne's Elegy.' It starts, 'My prime of youth is but a frost of cares.' He was only about twenty-five." I suddenly re-membered that Chidiock Tichborne had been caught because an injured leg stopped him from fleeing with his co-conspirators, and paused.

"How's he fit in with our bride?"

"He doesn't, but it's interesting. Context."

"Luke."

The toast popped up, so I filled the rack and grinned a little sheepishly. "Sorry. So Ginevra married Antony Tichborne on Christmas Eve 1641. I couldn't find any report of what happened to her, but I came across a couple of references to 'his tragic match' and his 'lost bride.' By itself, not much, but given that, well, we've met her...."

"You'd think it would be newsworthy, something like that."

"In any other year, maybe."

"What happened in 1641?"

"Trouble, and it got worse. 1642 is the start of the Civil War."

"Roundheads and Cavaliers, right? The king hiding up a tree."

I laughed. "That one, yeah. Except it was a lot grimmer in reality. You've got a king who's run the country into the ground, a financial crisis, religious extrem-ists on both sides, the beginnings of modern weaponry but no modern med-icine, and a conflict where people chose sides town by town, sometimes fam-ily by family. The royalists had cavalry, but no discipline, and parliament had the more disciplined army but less resources, at least at first. The man who was your neighbour before the war could well be standing behind a cannon blasting down your walls. There's a reason so few of our old castles are standing. Hell, they took on a good few churches and cathedrals as well."

Jay's eyes had gone wide and distant. "Got it. Seen civil wars. Hard to imag-ine it here, though."

"Yeah." I got up to refill my coffee and paused by the window, looking out at the quiet of the morning, the trees rising up and the mist curling off the lake. It was hard to imagine that there could ever have been battles here, but the local heaths had soaked up more than their share of blood before that particular war was done. Taking a slow breath, I said, "Young Antony joined the Royalist army. Easy to see why. Staunch Catholic, probably young and romantic, if he managed to sweep a beauty like Ginevra off her feet, still mourning his vanished wife—"

"You can't know this."

"No," I agreed, but I thought maybe I could. It was easy to imagine the dashing young cavalier riding down over the heath to pledge his sword to his king. The sandy soil would have flown up behind his horse's hooves, blurring the air behind him. Had he looked back at the hall from the next ridge? Had he thought of her as he rode away? How long had he searched for his missing foreign bride before he flung himself into war? Had he assumed that she had run away, scared by the looming war, or had he thought her kidnapped or lost in an accident? Shrugging off the thoughts, I continued, "He was a cavalry officer. Distinguished himself at Roundway Down. Somehow he ended up at the Battle of Alton."

Jay put his cup down hard. "Our Alton?"

"Been there?" It was ten miles away, on the other side of Aldershot's older and snootier sister town, Farnham. These days, Alton was a sleepy commuter town with a half-hearted tourist industry based on Jane Austen, who had lived nearby, and its heritage railway.

"Steam trains," he said, rolling his eyes slightly.

"Of course."

"Big bus rally, too, in the summer. Nice little place."

"Not in December 1643." I tried to think of some local landmarks that would help him. "You know the castle in Farnham, yeah? That was a parliamentary stronghold, and they wanted to control the land between there and Basingstoke. Imagine Major General Waller marching out of Farnham with five thousand men—"

"Down the middle of the A31?" His tone was light, but he'd stopped eating his toast.

"No. He took them due west, as if he was heading straight to Basingstoke, and then turned south in the middle of the night to come at Alton through the woods. They were using leather guns, which only need one horse to pull them, and there was a hard frost. No mud to slow them. They came in from the west just after dawn. Alton had a small garrison, cavalry and infantry. The cavalry broke out, headed for Winchester, supposedly for reinforcements—"

"And left the infantry?" I had all of Jay's attention now. "How many of them?"

"Somewhere between six and eight hundred of them. The parliamentary forces gradually drove them back until they were forced to take shelter around St. Lawrence's Church. They held their ground for two hours, firing out the windows and from behind a fortification just outside, but eventually they were forced inside. Our Tichborne was there, as well as the infantry colonel, Richard Boles. He's supposed to have said that he'd run through the first of his men who tried to surrender. All this while the Parliamentarians are hurling grenades through the windows. The Royalists didn't even have time to bolt the doors behind them before they were overwhelmed. Their last defence was a breast-work—well, pile, really—of dead horses in the middle of the church. Boles and Tichborne both went down there, poor bastards, fighting to the last."

I stopped, aware I'd got carried away with the story. Jay took a slow breath and said, "And that was that."

"Yeah. 13th December 1643." I got up to make more toast.

"Outlived her by less than two years."

"And here's the thing. He was a cavalry officer. He should have bolted with the rest of them, but he chose to stand and fight instead. He must have defied a direct order to do it, which is pretty typical of Royalist cavalry, to be honest. Hell, he could have just run for home. He was a local boy. If anyone could have escaped in the chaos, it would have been him."

"He didn't have anything to live for," Jay concluded quietly.

"The king wrote to his father to praise his heroism. I found a picture online of a memorial stone for them all in the church in Alton. Put after the Interregnum, of course."

"How old was he?"

"Twenty-two. She was seventeen when they got married."

He nodded, but didn't make any of the usual comments about how shocking their youth was. I guess he knew better than I that wars are always fought by ardent boys. What he did say, after a moment, was, "You didn't learn all that this morning."

I shrugged, a little embarrassed. "Military historian, even if it's not my period. I used to play Roundheads versus Cavaliers in the back garden as a kid, and I was a bit obsessed with all the battlefield histories in my teens. Alton was a bit of a byword for brutality, so it appealed to my spotty oik of a teenage self."

"Were you a Roundhead or a Cavalier?"

"Roundhead, always. Katie had to be the Cavalier. I made her dress up in a frilly shirt and stand in the paddling pool while I bombarded her with a Super Soaker. So I knew who Antony Tichborne was already, though not that he'd been married. Once I had his name, the rest was easy."

"What happened after he was killed?"

"Old Sir Walter died the next year. The hall went to the oldest son, but he fled to France during the Interregnum. He died out there, but he married a French girl first. Their son came back with Charles II and took the house on, but by then it's unlikely that anyone cared about what had happened to poor little Ginevra."

"Did she not have family?"

"I'm still trying to work out the Italian stuff. If I've picked through it right, her father was sent back to Genoa when the war broke out. He died in 1656, probably of plague, since half of Genoa died of it that year, and left no other issue."

"Makes you glad to live now," Jay said.

"Doesn't it," I agreed. "There were probably stories passed down, and once the Mistletoe Bride legend became so popular a few centuries later, someone reattached it to the old tale of the girl who went missing on her wedding night, especially with that painting and whatever she's been whispering in people's dreams for however long."

"Anything in your research to suggest they ever found her?"

"No." She was only a name and a few dates, a passing reference in a letter or two. She had left very little mark on history, and I thought of that other Tichborne, the one who had gone to his grave fifty years before her, lamenting his missed chances on the eve of his execution. *My tale was heard and yet it was not told*, he had written. *I saw the world and yet I was not seen.*

"So now what?" Jay asked.

I looked down at my toast, aware that he might not react well. "Now I go back to work."

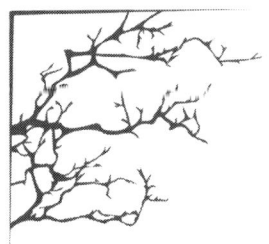

Chapter Eleven

Jay was not impressed, but I won out, mostly by pure persistence and reassuring him over and over that I wasn't scared at all. I admit, though, that I was a little apprehensive when I walked back into the hall. I stood in the library for a few minutes before I gave in and went to look at her portrait again. By day, light fell in through the cupola window above, and the painting sank back into the shadows a little. Her beauty was still striking, though, and I could see the white gleam of her dress out of the corner of my eye until I left the foyer.

Back in the library, I set to work with a vim. I had maybe one more day's worth of cataloguing to do, and then I could start packing up crates. I agreed with Jay on this—the sooner I was done, the better.

At first I was braced for any sound. None came. The sunshine kept streaming through the windows, and the heating pipes gurgled a little, but there were no footsteps. Eventually, I put some music on to keep me company, the local radio, in all its brash, advert-heavy, poppy good cheer. It was an old trick I'd used at Oxford, a way to ground myself in the ordinary world again when I was in danger of getting lost in my own head, and I was soon singing along cheerfully.

I ate my lunch sitting at the window table, watching a robin hop through the vines outside and cock its head at me through the window.

Not long after lunch, my phone rang. I glanced at it and saw that it was my mum. I was making good progress at last, and I knew that Mum would talk at me for an hour if I picked up, so I ignored it. I'd call her back later, while I was waiting for Jay to get back.

I got a lot done, though I was very conscious of the fading light.

When I heard the first footsteps upstairs, it was almost a relief. She was in the upstairs corridor again, outside the room where I had been staying. I had to go up into the gallery to fetch some books, and I could hear her more and more clearly as I stood on the other side of the door. I thought of the story I had pieced together that morning and closed my eyes, sadness washing over me. At that moment, I wasn't afraid of her. All I felt was pity.

"*Buonasera*, Ginevra," I murmured.

Yes, it was stupid.

The footsteps stopped, and the air seemed to gather around me, tight and heavy. Only then did it occur to me that it might be a bad idea to call her attention down on me.

I moved, stumbling into the desk as I grabbed the books I wanted and hurried down the stairs. At the bottom, I dropped back into the chair behind the desk, clutching its worn plastic arms, and took a deep breath.

Behind me, in the shadows, so did she.

I froze.

The sound of breathing stopped.

I sat in perfect stillness for a few more minutes before I remembered the lights and leaped up frantically to wave at them.

Outside there was the rumble of tires on gravel, and the lights of Jay's car swung across the window. I grabbed my stuff and bolted for the door.

Behind me, somewhere in the stacks, she sighed.

The library lights were still on when I hauled open the passenger door and threw myself in. I slammed the door behind me, and Jay said, "Having fun with the ghost?"

The lights flickered out, and he started back down the drive. I sighed in relief and said, "It was fine until it started getting dark."

"Can you get it done on time if you only work in daylight?"

"If I start earlier, maybe."

I didn't talk about the ghost or my work for the rest of the evening. We talked about Jay's day a little as we cooked, shared a meal, and then settled down in front of his telly again. I read. He watched a superhero film I'd seen posters for earlier in the year but never felt like seeing.

Well, we started out that way, at least. We actually spent most of the evening making out on the sofa. It was nice, and it was easy. That might not seem very exciting, but I relished it. Everything had felt so complicated for so long that easy was a blessing.

I didn't try to see him stripped completely bare that night, but turned my back politely until he switched the light off and reached for me. As I rose into his kiss, it occurred to me that this was the third night in a row I'd spent in his bed. There had been a time when I would have laughed myself sick at the idea of falling into bed with a near stranger and staying for days, but it didn't feel like a foolish impulse right then. Jay was a decent guy, we were both attracted to one another, and circumstances had chased me out of my own bed. There was no reason not to take pleasure in each other. Maybe we'd see each other after I'd finished my work here. Maybe we wouldn't. I hadn't had the best of luck when it came to serious relationships, and I wasn't looking for another one. I just liked him.

It was as easy as that.

Jay's just informed me that I'm a crappy liar, and it was completely obvious that I was smitten. If I was, I was the last to know.

What do you mean "as usual." Git. Just because you couldn't resist my many charms. Go away and let me write in peace.

Or take the other end of the sofa and let me write in peace. That's fine too. Better, in fact, because I can look at you when I'm searching for words. You can't see the screen anymore, so I'll just have to tell you this later. I'm not convinced I was smitten with you quite that soon, but I am now. Irrevocably so.

So, life at Eelmoor Hall fell into a sort of routine. I woke up early, went for a run if the weather permitted, then moved over to the hall until the sun started to set, when I'd walk back to Jay's. The weather had turned dull and the clouds covered the sky without a break, making it hard to keep track of time. It rained some days, but never for more than an hour. A few times the rain turned to thick sleet, but each time it eventually faded back into drizzle again. I worked steadily, filling crates and stacking them along the walls as I cleared each set of shelves. The library grew a little more empty and echoing by the day.

There were a few things I omitted to tell Jay about my days. We talked about a lot that week, usual getting-to-know-you stuff. I learned about his mum and sister back in Ballymena, and how he no longer felt he had much in common with them. I told him stories from my and Katie's childhood, about growing up in a seaside town. He talked about his plans for when this job ended in the spring, how he needed to find a flat and start his civilian life properly, and I chattered about some of the places I'd lived, how I was sick of the centre of London and its constant racket.

I didn't tell him that for an hour each day, once I'd eaten my lunch, I was exploring the rest of the hall, looking for the missing chest. I'd managed to track down an online copy of a history of the house written in the 1840s by the baronet of that time, which sternly demolished the legend of the Mistletoe Bride and mentioned that the replica chest had been designed in accordance with Italian fashions of Ginevra's era. Sir John referred to her, with all the pomposity of his era, as "that piteous runaway, who faced with the fear of persecution, no doubt gave in to the innate impulsivity of her Mediterranean nature." He couldn't account for what had become of the original chest, although he did mention it had been part of her trousseau. I thought that was probably nonsense. If they really knew what chest she was in, she would have been found. I did wonder if Sir John had something else right, though. Had she regretted her engagement? Threatened to run away? Was that why they had stopped looking for her so soon? It was impossible to know, all these centuries later.

I hadn't realized just how huge the main house was until I tried to explore every room. I started in the more deserted corners, checking store cupboards and box rooms, but soon found myself simply wandering through conference rooms and solemn wood-panelled offices and along twisting little stairways that connected up the floors in unexpected ways. I found an entire gym in the west wing with rows of machines sitting untouched and the dust beginning to fuzz over their seats, and a room stuffed full of resuscitation dummies tumbled together in big wire racks. There were two hundred bedrooms in the main house alone, and I checked every one of them as well as all the cleaning cupboards and cubbyholes in between. I was steadily working my way up towards the attic, which I dreaded a little. It was bad enough wandering these echoing rooms when they had sunlight streaming through the windows. I was certain there would be no such kindly light in the roof space.

Because that was the other thing I'd decided Jay was better off not knowing—I wasn't walking those halls alone. Every step I took had an echo, faint but there, and every time I stopped to check it wasn't just my imagination, I could hear her breathing just behind my shoulder. It made my spine clench every time, but there was none of that unbearable midnight terror, so I gritted my teeth and tried to pretend she wasn't there.

Days blurred together, soft and grey and haunted. By day I packed crates and hunted for another kind of box entirely. By night I drifted into Jay's orbit and he anchored me somehow, brought me out of that strange reverie in which I spent my days. Mark texted me a few times, asking me what I was up to, but I couldn't think of the right words to explain the weirdness of Eelmoor Hall and so left them unanswered. My mum phoned again, but I'd forgotten to phone her back the first time and didn't feel up to even her gentle brand of guilt trip. I let it ring quiet, its echoes fading into the greyness of my mind.

I forgot to check my e-mails, and left my phone on Jay's kitchen table during the day when its constant beeping and vibrating started annoying me.

By then I was talking to her as we searched the halls. My lunchtime hunts had stretched into entire afternoons, though I was still packing books in the mornings. We'd got up to the third floor, one below the attics, and the quiet sat heavy in the air there. I told her the story of the Battle of Alton, just like I'd told Jay, and heard her catch her breath when I explained how her Antony had died, fighting to the last.

I was feeling tired and light-headed, muzzy from the stuffy atmosphere and the weight of sorrow in the air. We'd made it to the bottom of the attic stairs, but I didn't want to take that first step up into the darkness. I felt a little like I was dreaming, or very, very drunk, but some part of me still rebelled against the darkness. I sat down on the steps instead, leaning my head against the wall.

"Poor Tony," she whispered, settling beside me. I could almost imagine that I saw her. I definitely sensed movement through the air.

She leaned her head against my shoulder, soft curls brushing my cheek, and sighed again. She felt no colder than the air, which was winter bitter, and I sighed too, my breath steaming slightly.

Slow exhaustion settled over me again, sinking into me like the cold. It felt like the days just after Danny went missing, when I was still dazed from the concussion and too bewildered to understand why my whole life had just fallen into pieces. I'd felt so grey then, as if there wasn't even meant to be colour in the world, and I felt it again there in Eelmoor Hall, sitting on the stairs with the ghost of somebody else's lost lover.

I closed my eyes.

I must have slept, though I don't remember much of my dreams, just endless shadowy corridors meeting at strange angles: the hall, my old school, the Exam Schools in Oxford, the history department of my university, ancient and modern entangled. I remember the smell of pines, a distant whisper of music.

All the time, I could hear her whispering, though it took me a while to realize what she was doing.

She was counting down from one hundred.

Footsteps went scattering ahead of me, always just around the corner, and I heard laughter, bright and sweet. Doors slammed, stairs creaked, smothered giggles drifted out of cupboards and corners. There was no one there, though. They were all invisible.

Or maybe I was.

"Seventy-three."

A movement caught my eye at the end of the hall, a flash of a candle lighting. For a moment I saw Danny standing there, the candle flame illuminating his golden hair, but then he pinched the candle out and we were back in the maze of shadows again. I went running after him, but when I reached the end of the corridor there was no one there and no way out.

"Seventy-two."

There was a chest, though, a big wooden chest with its lid hanging open. Maybe he was in there. Maybe he was going to jump out and surprise me.

I leaned forward to look.

"Luke!"

It was Jay's voice, loud and frantic, and it made me jerk back from the chest.

"Luke! Wake up!"

I hadn't even realized I was still asleep. That was enough to jolt me out of the dream, and I opened my eyes.

I was still sitting on the stairs, though the sky outside was dark now. Jay stood in front of me, gripping his torch in one hand even though the lights were on.

"Hi," I said, and the word was clumsy in my mouth. I still felt like I was dreaming, everything a little grey and floating around me.

"You okay?"

"Just sat down for a few moments. Hi."

"Said that already." He was still looking worried. "Let's get out of here."

"Okay," I said, but I couldn't find it in myself to move. My feet didn't quite feel part of me.

Up in the darkness at the top of the attic stairs, Ginevra whispered, *"Seventy-one."*

Jay tensed. "Luke?"

"Mmm." My eyes were falling closed again.

"What's she doing?"

"Counting down," I told him. Wasn't it obvious? The dream was rising up around me again.

"What happens when she gets to zero?"

His voice cut through my haze, and I opened my eyes again. I smiled at him a little dreamily. "She'll come looking for me, of course, whether I'm ready or not."

"Okay. Right. Shit. *Luke*! Honey, I need you to stay awake and with me, okay?"

I'd been drifting again, but the endearment sounded so out of place from him that it woke me up, and I smiled. "That's nice. Sweet. 'Honey,' I mean."

"Got it." He looked down at me, and his eyes were creased with worry even though his voice was light. "Okay, I can't lift you to carry you out of here, so I need you to help me."

"Course. Anything to help."

"Seventy," she whispered, a little closer to the head of the stairs.

"Stand up for me," Jay said and then added, a little awkwardly, "Honey."

It was hard, my mind not quite connecting with my body, but that last word had been sweet and hilarious enough to inspire me. I pulled myself up the wall, and he grabbed my hand.

"You're cold."

"No, I'm not," I said vaguely. "Not even shivering, see."

"Not reassuring. Walk with me. Just to the lift."

I hung back. I didn't want to go up into that darkness, but I couldn't leave by myself. "Danny."

"What about him?" Jay tugged at my hand, coaxing me a few steps on.

"Shouldn't leave him up here with the ghost."

"Danny's not here."

"I saw him."

Jay kept moving, his hand locked so tightly around mine that I had to either go with him or pull him over. "You were dreaming, honey. Come on."

I let him hustle me into the lift, where he jabbed at the buttons and then embraced me. He felt fever hot, and I shuddered against him, my body realizing that I was cold, so very cold.

Jay wrapped me in his jacket, kissed me, and then held on again. "How long have you been up there?"

"I just had lunch," I mumbled, putting my head on his shoulder. I still felt out of sync with the world, and the shudders that were beginning to wrack me were just making it worse.

He caught my hands, rubbing warmth back into them. "It's after nine. I've been looking for you for the last two hours."

"Sorry. Never meant to put you out. Must have just closed my eyes."

"With a bit of help, aye? Thought she'd gone quiet too easily."

The lift stopped, and the doors slid open to the ground floor corridor. It felt warmer down here, and I began to shiver hard, my feet and hands tingling. "Warm."

"Heating's off on the top floors. Just had it on for the library wing. I'm parked outside the north foyer, okay? Can you manage it? For me."

I nodded and clung to his hand, every step unsteady. I felt like I was drunk, the bad kind where you suddenly stand up at the end of the evening and realize how much you've had and that you don't know how you're going to get home.

Halfway down the corridor, her steps began to echo behind us, softly keeping pace.

At the door out of the north foyer, a wave of dizziness swept over me, and I had to sit down hard, dropping my head into my hands.

"*Sixty-five,*" Ginevra whispered from the dark corner under the stairs.

"Luke," Jay said softly. "Come on now."

I managed to stagger to my feet, but I froze in the doorway. I couldn't leave the hall, not when Danny was lost in there, not when I still needed to find the box. It would be wrong to walk out.

"Honey," Jay said, sounding desperate. "Sweetheart, darling, hot stuff, babe, lover. Come on. Fuck it, Luke, I'm running out of words. Don't make me try German. I only know stupid ones in German."

"Didn't know you spoke it," I protested, dragging my thoughts away from the darkness upstairs.

"Everyone who's been posted out there speaks enough to get laid. *Liebling.*"

"Sixty-four."

"*Schatzi*," Jay said fiercely. He could have been swearing at me for all I knew, but it helped, and I shuffled forward another step. "*Schnucki, kuschelbär*, Luke, will you get *out* of there."

I made a last effort and threw myself through that open doorway. Jay slammed the door behind me. I staggered down towards the car. It did feel easier to move out here, but I was still shivering.

"Get in the car and I'll put the heating on." He came round and opened the door for me, leaning over to switch on the ignition and heating before he headed round to his own side. He pulled himself in and reached over to pull me into a tight hug again. "Do I need to be driving you to A&E?"

"I'm fine," I tried to tell him. "Just need to warm up, and your place is closer."

"Got a blanket in the back, if you need it."

"Cup of tea would help more."

He nodded and reached down to switch his leg off. "Let's go, then."

And from the back seat, Ginevra said, *"Sixty-three."*

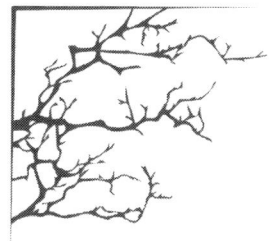

Chapter Twelve

Jay's hands tightened on the wheel, and he said, "Get the fuck out of my car, bitch."

His voice was quiet, but his tone made me flinch back into my seat. It clearly scared Ginevra as well, because there was an immediate shift in the atmosphere. My head cleared further, more of the clouds dissolving.

"Huh," Jay said. "Didn't really expect that to work."

I glanced at him sideways as we drove off, and could just pick out the edge of a satisfied smile.

So I got warm tingles in my belly. Sue me. I was off-balance anyway, and here he was, this guy. Jay McBride, who kept rescuing me.

"You still awake there?"

"Just about."

"Don't doze off. Keep talking."

"I'm fine."

"It's well below freezing. You've been sitting on an unheated staircase for eight hours. In a T-shirt."

"I was moving boxes around all morning. People don't realize how heavy books are."

"Yeah?"

"And I forgot to put my jacket back on when I went for my lunchtime wander. My bad."

"Been many lunchtime wanders?"

I went quiet. He'd made it pretty clear that he thought my determination to find her was stupid, and I didn't want to hear him get angry with me or, much worse, to be afraid for me.

"Luke?" We were drawing up outside his building, and it was a relief to see the kitchen lights blazing out.

"I'm awake."

"Inside, then."

I was still shivering when we got inside, but he chivvied me through onto the sofa and then deposited the double duvet on top of me. "Wrap up."

I did as I was told as he went back to the kitchen. I'd just managed to snuggle down properly when he returned with a big cup of milky tea complete with three chocolate Hobnobs balanced on the edge of the plate. I sat up and drank it down meekly while he scowled at me.

"You look like shit."

"Cheers."

"Still not convinced I shouldn't just drive you to hospital."

"No!" I couldn't leave, not yet. I shouldn't even be this far away from the hall, not when I still hadn't found her.

That thought was creepy enough to make me stop and reconsider. When had I last left the grounds of Eelmoor Hall? Jay had been picking up groceries on the way home from work, which meant I didn't need to, so it must have been New Year's Eve, which had been about a week ago.

It was only then that I realized that I had no idea what the date was.

"Jay?"

"Yeah." He was rubbing my leg through the duvet but listening to the microwave whir more than me.

"What's the date?"

"Sixteenth."

"Really?" It came out much more sharply than I intended. He turned to look at me, concerned again.

"Yeah. What's going on?"

I closed my eyes and actually thought about it, trying to work out the reasoning behind everything I'd done in the last week. (The last fortnight, that was. Shit.)

"I think she got in my head again," I admitted.

He nodded and stood up. "Come and eat. Talk it through."

He'd heated up soup, and I devoured it gladly, shaking my head at the beer he offered. When I'd taken the edge off my hunger, I sat back a little. "I've been looking for the chest."

"Thought you were going to focus on work."

"It was just in my lunch break." I sighed. "And then my afternoons."

He looked down at his empty bowl. "You didn't mention it."

"No." I got up and took the bowls over to the sink. The soup was sitting warmly in my belly, but I still didn't feel right. "It was my decision, even if you think it was a stupid—"

"Of course it was. Would just have been nice to know."

"And what? Spend our evenings stressing about it? She was always going to turn up again, whether I went looking or not."

He regarded me across the table, that steady unreadable look that I was getting used to. He said, "I could have helped."

"What?"

He frowned a little. "I still think it was a bad call, but it was yours to make. So why not ask for help?"

I just stared at him. It had never occurred to me. "I... I just... I never...."

"Ask? Why not?" He came over to stand behind me and added hesitantly, "This thing—us, whatever it is—it means you can ask."

I closed my eyes. "Honestly, this, well, us, makes asking harder. It's—look, I had to teach myself to put stuff in boxes. Not actual boxes, obviously, and not actual stuff, either, but.... I used to imagine I had a big marker pen and was drawing lines across my life. I had my day and my work and stuff I'd seen, and I couldn't tell Danny about it, because I never knew what was going to set him off. If I had a bad day, or too good a day, or I mentioned that someone else had good news, it all pushed him off balance, and then—"

"He'd hurt you."

I laughed bitterly. "No. He hit me *once*, and it was the thing that finally made him run. He hurt *himself*. A lot, and I—I couldn't bear it. So I learned to smile and keep quiet about—" I shrugged.

"Everything that mattered to you?"

"He mattered more. I... I used to be able to smile through anything. *Anything*. I thought it was the only bloody skill I brought out of all that. I don't know why I can't do it anymore." I was shaking again, and I turned into him in relief when he wrapped his arms around me. "Damn it. I usually have more of a backbone than this, I promise."

He rubbed my back and said, "Right. Here's what we're going to do. Tonight, you're getting into bed and warming up. Extra blankets. Hot water bottle."

"You?" I asked hopefully.

"Me. Tomorrow, we go and find that box. And then it's done."

"What, just like that?"

"Quicker with help. For instance, could have told you she wouldn't be on the third floor. Fire in the eighties. All got remodelled. If she was there, they would have found her then."

"Or moved her," I said, pieces suddenly clicking into place in my mind. "Places like this, old places, they get remodelled all the time. Whole rooms vanish sometimes—get walled up or blocked in. But a fire would mean they moved stuff in a hurry, even stuff that had been lost for centuries."

"I only know that there was a fire," Jay said. "The old caretaker didn't tell me any details beyond that."

"She wanted me to go into the attic."

"Haven't been up there. Sounds like a good place to start."

I swallowed hard. "She follows me around while I'm looking."

"Course she does." He sighed. "We watch out for each other up there, yeah?"

"Yeah," I said, trying and failing to sound as nonchalant as him.

Okay, so by this point, I probably *was* smitten, whether I knew it or not. Can you blame me?

I was still feeling limp and shivery, so I was glad when he chased me into bed. He actually did bring me a hot water bottle, one with a fluffy cover printed with pink teddy bears.

He saw me biting back laughter and said, "My sister let my niece pick her own Christmas presents."

"How old is she?"

"Six."

"Cute." I lifted up the duvet so he could slide it in below my feet and waggled my eyebrows at him. "And you."

I was getting dangerously addicted to snuggling with Jay McBride. At the time, I thought it was just the aftermath of an emotional day, something that I could easily do without when I went back to my normal life. I was so wrong. I'm still addicted. No one in the world could possibly cuddle as well as Jay. (Jealous? Tough shit. He's mine.)

"There's fifty-three missed calls on your phone."

"Shit. Mum rang the other day. I meant to call her back. It's Dad's birthday next week." I didn't want to move, not when his arm was looped loosely around my waist and I was perfectly comfortable against him. "Tomorrow. After we've finished this."

He nodded, and I relaxed further. "I told Ginevra about her husband. How he died, I mean."

"Yeah?" His hand stilled on my back.

"She spoke to me. 'Poor Tony,' she said."

"To you?"

"Yeah. She sounded so sad. I mean, I get that she's put me in danger, but I still feel bad for her. I think she loved him."

Jay was staring at me. "She called you by his name? By the name of the guy who left her in a box to die?"

"It sounds a lot less romantic when you put it like that," I complained.

"You see too much good in people."

I shook my head at that, a little irritated. "I'm not naive."

Jay kissed the top of my head lightly. "Didn't say you were."

"Plenty have." It always grated, mostly because it nearly always came from people whose idea of a bad breakup involved commitment issues and tubs of chocolate ice cream rather than multiple emergency services.

"I won't."

No, I don't deserve him. Never did. Doesn't mean I'm willing to give him up.

"London to Aldershot isn't that far by train," I said. "When this is all over, how about we share a meal that neither of us had to cook?"

"Love to," he said and chuckled. "Don't expect me to put out until the third date, though."

I smiled against his chest. "You're so straitlaced, Jay. How am I ever going to get you naked?"

He slid his hand up beneath my T-shirt. "Feeling warm again. How about you demonstrate this naked thing?"

I still felt like a limp noodle, but that deserved a little appreciation. I pulled myself up enough to peel off my T-shirt and wriggled round in his lap. He ran an appreciative hand down my spine, and I sighed and slumped forward against him, burying my face against his neck. He was so warm and comfortable. It would be so easy just to slide into sleep like this, cocooned in the duvet and his warm arms.

"Luke?"

"Mmm." His hand had stopped, and I pulled my head back a little, remembering what I'd started. "Oh, sorry." I turned my chin just enough to kiss his throat.

He put his hands on my shoulders and eased me back, frowning down at me. "Not a rewards program."

"What?"

"You don't need to earn points." He pulled me back down against his shoulder, wrapping his arms around me tightly when I tried to move. "Stop squirming, Luke."

"But—"

"Prefer my lovers fully conscious. And into it."

"I am—"

He actually ruffled my hair. "It's *fine*. Go back to sleep."

"I do want you." I was feeling anxious now, a sickly familiar twist of panic in my gut. I needed him to believe it enough to stick around.

He sighed. "Your ex was an arsehole."

That annoyed me. "He was not. He couldn't help—"

"Not saying he didn't have a good excuse. Doesn't mean he was right in the way he treated you. Definitely doesn't mean you should expect the same from everyone."

I managed to pull out of his arms enough to scowl at him. "You have no idea. You're not being fair."

He looked back at me. "Reckon it was like this—he came home sometimes, drunk probably, maybe high, and woke you up, demanded sex. You were glad enough to see him home in one piece that you went with it."

"He never forced me," I said through stiff lips.

"I get that. Never asked if you wanted it, either, did he?"

I stared at him. How could he know? How could he possibly know? There were things I'd never told anyone—not Mark, not Katie, not any of the friends who had stuck around. There were things no one else needed to know, things you did for someone you loved that I was afraid would seem trivial to anyone who hadn't been there, no matter that the scars they left had taken the longest to heal.

"Seen a lot of bad divorces," Jay said softly, watching me. "Been to a fuckton of group therapy. Guessing you haven't?"

"Haven't what?"

"Therapy."

"No." I was shaking too hard to say more, let alone the usual obvious responses—it had been ten years, I hadn't been the one who really needed the help, I wanted it behind me, not to have to go wallowing through it again.

"Worth a thought." He held out his arm. "Hey."

I dived for him. He hugged me tight again. I shook against him for a while, so many thoughts tangling in my mind that I couldn't chop them up enough to say them out loud.

"Sorry," Jay murmured. "Shouldn't have gone there. Hey, you're okay. You're good."

I nodded and choked out, "Don't worry."

He huffed out a dry laugh, shaking his head. "Shit, you... I'm sorry."

I was shuddering less with each slow stroke of his hand along my back, sinking back down against him. "S'okay. Haven't melted down for a while. Thought I was past that." Suddenly aware that I was picking up his speech patterns, I made the next bit a full sentence. "It was a long time ago, and I was sure I was ready to move on. I guess it's never quite that easy."

"No. There was a guy I knew, at Bastion. Engine caught fire while he was working on it. Threw his arms up over his face as it went up. Third degree burns. He said he didn't realize how bad it was at first. His hands were wrecked, but he thought his arms were just a bit red and sore. Said he was well pissed off when they told him all that skin had to come off as well, to stop the layer below from getting infected. Better in the long run, though. No gangrene."

"I don't have emotional gangrene," I said. "Gross."

"Still. Have to clean it out properly."

"Yeah," I said bitterly. "Bloody ghost is helping with that."

His arms tightened around me. After a moment he said, "Probably better off with the NHS."

It startled a laugh out of me. "Yeah, not sure I trust her qualifications."

We lay around for a while longer, talking about inconsequential things, until I dozed off on his shoulder. I woke up when he moved me.

"Just going to lock up. Back soon."

I probably mumbled something at him. I'm sure I rolled into the warm patch he'd left in the pillow, letting my eyes fall shut again as I listened to him move around. When I heard him undressing, something struck me as odd, but it wasn't until I heard the soft beep of the charger connecting that I realized what it was.

The bedside lamp was still on.

"Lights," I reminded him.

"It's okay."

I opened my eyes as he sat on the bed beside me and caught my breath.

He was naked, completely naked. His shortened thigh was closer to me, out in plain sight, and he didn't move to cover it as I looked his way. Instead he repeated, "It's okay."

It was. After the way he had kept it hidden, I had been braced for awful scars. There were none. It was narrower than his muscled right thigh, and ended sooner, but that was it. The end was covered over with skin, perfectly smooth. I reached out, and he didn't stop me, but just drew a breath in slowly when I cupped my hand around his stump.

"Does it hurt?" I asked.

"Not to touch. Sore, sometimes. Takes the brunt of walking." He grimaced. "Foot on that side hurts at times. Less than it used to."

I'd read about phantom pain but hadn't applied that knowledge to Jay. "Must feel weird."

"Yeah." He was looking at me, his eyes wide, so I leaned forward to kiss him gently. His breath gusted out against my mouth, pure relief.

I needed to be clear, though. "No point-collecting on your side, either. I mean, just because you've seen my weak spots doesn't mean you're obliged to—"

He cut me off with a finger on my lips. "Not like that." He pulled back, flopping down against the pillows. "C'mere."

I dropped down beside him, propping myself up on one elbow so I could see his face. He looked very faraway, his eyes sad, but then he focused on me again. "Sounds like you never gave up on your guy."

"For all the good it did us."

He touched my mouth again, pressing my lips still with the pad of his fingers. "I was seeing someone. Before."

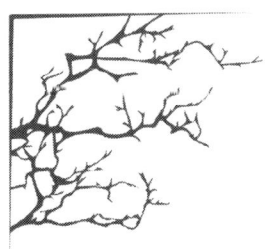

Chapter Thirteen

M y first reaction was to be furious at myself. I'd looked at him, seen his leg, and assumed that was the whole story. Then I looked down at him again and forgot about that. I wanted to listen to him. I could scold myself later.

"Was it serious?"

"Not quite. Could have been, if I'd been home more. We were talking about it. We were both out, but not shouting it out, see. Out if anyone thought to ask."

"Got it."

"He was a civilian. Couldn't share army housing unless we got a civil partnership. Not really ready for that, so it would have meant private housing. Would have been a big deal. Even so, we were thinking about it." He shrugged a little.

"Sounds serious to me."

"Maybe." The sadness was back in his eyes. "Came to see me while I was still in Birmingham. Told me he didn't think he was strong enough to support me through such a traumatic time, so he'd decided it was kinder to make a clean break of it. Didn't want to have to let me down later."

"Fucking bastard." It was my first instinctive reaction, and I said it before I stopped to think that Jay might not appreciate hearing it about someone he'd cared for.

He smiled, just slightly. "Pretty much what I said. Got a bit ugly then."

"I'd have made him a bit ugly. What a dick."

Jay's smile grew a little sheepish. "Hit him with my crutch."

I choked a little. "Seriously?"

"Got him in the nuts. Bit stupid, really. He could have pressed charges. Was on quite a lot of painkillers, though. Not thinking straight."

"How soon after you got back to the UK was this?" I demanded.

He turned his face away from me a little. "Couple of days. They escorted him out of the ward, and no one said anything. Guess they see a lot of that kind of thing up there."

The first thing I felt was anger—sheer, blazing, shaking anger. I wanted to find the bastard and hurt him enough that he knew what it felt like to be frightened and hurting and suddenly alone. I hadn't missed the way Jay carefully avoided his name, though, and I suspected I would never find out enough about him to actually track him down. (This, incidentally, wasn't quite true. It took Jay five years to tell me, but I know who he is now. Michael Robertson, if you're still out there, I hope someone cuts your dick off with a blunt spoon, you spineless dickhead.)

There was nothing I could do then except lean down and kiss Jay hard. "You deserve better."

"Yeah?" he murmured and brought his hands up to frame my face. It was a romantic gesture, and I both noticed that and was completely unfazed by it. I think by then it was beginning to dawn on me that here was the man I'd been vaguely dreaming about for years, the one who could be relied on no matter what.

"Yeah," I breathed and smiled down at him. "He was a fool to let you go. You're amazing."

He blushed, looking very uncomfortable. "Wasn't looking for sympathy. Just... you stuck around for Danny. Lot of people wouldn't have done."

"Lots of people are idiots," I pointed out and kissed him again. When he pulled me down, I went willingly, fitting between his legs like I belonged there, his right leg thrown over my hip and his bare thigh warm against my side. Now, flustered and thrilled by his honesty, I was turned on, wanting to touch every bit of him.

I could feel he was hard, even through my jeans, but he hesitated a little. It took me a moment to realize why, but when I did I pulled his hand across to press it against my erection. He moulded his hand around it, making me shiver, and smirked slowly.

"Want something?"

"You," I told him, pushing into his hand. "In me. Slow and steady."

His eyes were hot as he reached to undo my jeans. "I can do that."

As I went rolling across the bed with him, I couldn't help thinking that life was surprisingly good.

AND THEN, THAT NIGHT, I dreamed. It wasn't the usual nonsensical type of dream I'd had since leaving the main house. This one started with a sound I'll never be able to forget, that distinct crack of my own nose breaking as Danny hit me with a bottle. Then, on cue, the rush of pain rolled over me again.

I relieved it all, in a dream I couldn't escape, and this time I knew I was being watched. She was there, in the shadows behind the door, breathing a little fast as I screamed and dropped, my hands flying up to my face.

She was there in the cab too, sitting in the space beside me as we drove through a night that never seemed to end. I could feel the weight of her attention through the pain and the flash of streetlights through the window. The dream, like the night itself, broke into little glittering fragments—the gleam of the silent driver's gelled black hair, Danny crying, my hand curling in his hair, half in agony and half to tell him that he wasn't evil, he didn't deserve to die, stop saying that, please, please, please. Then the flash of blue lights outside the hospital, the fly-filled strip lighting inside, blood soaking into my shirt and the world throbbing around me, light to dark to light again.

And all through it, she was breathing in my ear, intent. I could almost feel her reaction, her fascination, and her delight.

And then I woke up, unable to move.

I was still in Jay's bed. I could still see the dim glow of his charger and the red numbers on his alarm clock. I wasn't back in the hall.

But I couldn't move. Worse, I could feel wood pressing against my hand where it was splayed across Jay's chest, trapping me in an invisible box.

I was still hoping it was just a lingering nightmare when the fear came.

It began, like before, at my toes, crawling up over me in a slow wave of horror. I could feel it in the air, pressing down on me heavily, until I had to gasp to get any air in at all. It built and built, and with it my panic grew. I knew now that I was trapped in here until I died, that I would never be free—of her, of Danny, of my regrets. My heart raced, my feet and hands began to cramp, and my breathing sped up. The faster and faster I breathed, the less air I could get in, until red shadows went swirling across my vision and I still couldn't breathe.

When the fear faded, I couldn't move, but my heart slowed, and I became aware of other things: the slow rise and fall of Jay's breathing, the tick of my watch on the bedside table, the warm sting of blood sliding down my knuckles.

The soft footsteps crunching on the gravel outside.

She'd found us.

The fear began again, worse than before.

This time it hurt, every breath I managed to gasp in rasping through my throat. My chest burnt and my head spun, and I couldn't move enough to scream. Just as it reached its peak, just as I started to crave anything that would make it *stop*, I felt Jay stir beside me.

"Luke?"

He switched the light on, and the fear immediately began to fade.

I still couldn't move, couldn't breathe, and outside, she was still walking through the darkness with a slow scrape of silk over gravel.

"Luke!"

The air was getting heavier and heavier, pressing down on my chest so hard it felt like concrete. I gasped again, trying to get just a little bit more air in, but it hurt so much and my whole body was locking up into one solid lump of pain, refusing to move, refusing to breathe. My vision was turning black, Jay's face swimming further and further away.

"Luke!" Even his voice seemed distant, but I heard her echo him clearly, soft and malicious.

"Luke. Poor Luke."

And I stopped breathing.

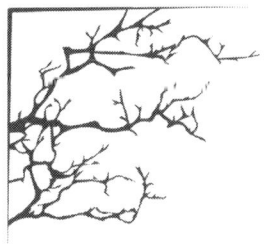

Chapter Fourteen

I woke up in hospital, with an aching chest and a breathing mask on my face. It was a shock to see white ceiling panels and bright lights, more so to have so many people around. I panicked a little, shoving the breathing mask off, and something started beeping. A nurse came bustling over, all brisk efficiency, and I stared at her in confusion. After weeks at Eelmoor Hall, this didn't feel real.

"I think I should be going now," I told her. "Do you know where I can get a cab?"

"Not until the doctor's seen you," she told me. "How are you feeling?"

"Weird," I said honestly, looking around. It really was a hospital, clean and sterile smelling, but with worn corners and cheap furniture. The plastic curtain was pulled along one side of the bed, but I could see it was a large ward, every bed full and medical staff moving in and out briskly. "Um, just so I'm sure, I am still alive, right?" Another thought occurred and I reached up to touch my nose, checking the break was healed. It was, which meant the last few years hadn't been a dream. All the same. "And it's 2014, right? No, 2015 now."

She smiled at me kindly. "You're in Frimley Park Hospital, bless you. You had a bit of a problem breathing in the night, and your friend called an ambulance. Are you feeling better?"

"Yes," I said slowly. It all seemed very prosaic, and the echo of that overwhelming fear was still very close. "Much. Thank you."

"Now you sit tight and try to relax. You can hang on to that mask. Just pop it back on if you start to struggle. I'll let the doctor know you're awake. Would you like your friend to come and sit with you?"

"Please."

Jay came in a few moments later. He'd managed to get dressed and put his leg back on, but his hair was sticking out in all directions as if he'd been running his hands through it. When he saw me sitting up, he smiled, eyes bright with relief.

Seeing him shook me a little. I had never been so glad to see someone in my life, and I didn't quite know what to do with it. Awkwardly I cleared my throat and said, "Thanks."

"Scared the fuck out of me." He hovered a step away, looking uncertain.

I held out my hand. "Come here. Please."

He stepped closer, pulling me into a tight hug. I leaned into him and re-laxed. It felt strange, strange but good, to have someone to lean on.

Someone cleared their throat politely, and Jay pulled back. It was a doctor, who wasn't even trying to hide her smile. "Right, then," she said. "Luke, is it? A few checks to see if you're back to your normal self before we decide whether to let you loose. If you want your friend—or is it partner—to stay, that's fine, but he doesn't have to."

"Do," Jay muttered.

"He can stay," I said.

"Fair enough. And just in case he hasn't told you, you should be very grate-ful to him. He did CPR until the ambulance came."

He shrugged a little, looking away, but I just stared at him. "Really? It was that bad? Jay—"

"Talk to the doctor, Luke."

She chuckled a little. "Let's see if we can work out just what went wrong for you. I need to check your blood pressure and have you blow into a tube, for a start. Any history of childhood asthma?"

"Me? No, but my sister had it. Didn't last."

"How old is she?" the doctor asked, wrapping the blood pressure tube around my upper arm.

"Twenty-six."

"Tell her to keep an eye on it. It can pop back up in your midtwenties. Any unusual stress or causes of anxiety in your life right now?"

"No," I said.

"Yes," Jay corrected and glared at me a little.

"Blood pressure's fine. Few more questions. Jay, you can tell me if he's lying again."

"Stress doesn't make me ill," I complained. "Just keeps me up at nights."

"And that's my next question."

I was pretty sure there was no medical explanation for ghost attacks, but I also wanted to get out of there, so I meekly answered the rest of her questions. She listened and nodded and then said, "Right. What I think happened was that you just had a bad asthma attack, brought on partly by how cold you were earlier in the evening and partly from a panic attack because of the sleep paralysis. I'm going to prescribe a couple of inhalers, and I want you to make an appointment to be checked by your GP so they can confirm the diagnosis and do some tests to rule out any sleep disorders. Can you do that?"

"Sure."

She looked past me to Jay. "Make sure he does."

"Will do."

"Can I leave now?" I asked, aware I was being petulant but a little annoyed at being briskly patronized

"You're good to go."

I sighed with relief, and Jay made things better by saying, "Got some clothes for you."

He'd also brought his car, to my relief. I hadn't fancied the wait for a taxi.

"Hop in."

I climbed in with relief and then turned to look at him. "Sounds nice and scientific, doesn't it? Asthma."

"Sounds plausible."

"Except you heard her too, didn't you? Ginevra."

"Yeah," he said. "I did. Sure you want to come back with me? Could take you to the station. Get you back to London safely."

"No," I said. I had no compassion left for her now, but I was angry. "She tried to kill me. Twice. I want to end this."

"How?"

"We give ourselves until noon to find her box. After that, Google for an exorcist."

"Tough talk. You believe in that?"

"Even if I don't, I bet she does. Good old-fashioned Catholic girl like that."

It was still dark, although the sun was beginning to show. Jay pulled off the motorway when we got to Farnborough, saying, "Wait for daylight. Breakfast?"

We feasted on bacon sandwiches and gritty coffee in a greasy spoon round the back of the industrial estate. Jay was obviously known here, because he got the odd nod and grunted greeting, but I got a few curious looks. I didn't care.

"Are you working today?" I said, suddenly thinking of it.

"Day off. Saturday. Might have called in anyway. This matters."

"Attics first?" I said, wiping my mouth with satisfaction.

"Yeah. Lift goes up that far."

I finished my coffee and sat back in my chair. "Anywhere else we should look?"

"There's a basement. Harness room above the old stables."

"Okay. Attics, basement, harness room, exorcism."

He quirked a grin at me over his cup. "Nice to-do list."

It was cold as we left the cafe, though the sun was up. The skies were heavy with cloud, and as we turned onto the road over the heath, it began to snow, wet splashes against the windscreen. Jay had put the radio on, and music pumped out, loud and fierce against the muted landscape.

When we got back to the gates of the hall, there was someone else parked outside, leaning out of the car window to press at the intercom.

Jay rolled down the window as he slowed to a stop. "Lost, folks?"

"This is Eelmoor Hall, right?"

I knew that voice, and I leaned past Jay to say, "Mark?"

Mark came shooting out of the car. "Luke? You're still here?"

"Yeah." I was confused. "Where else would I be?"

"And you're okay? Alive? Well? Capable of picking up a fucking phone?"

Oh.

Jay turned to me. "You know this guy?"

"He's Danny's brother. Family."

"Right." He leaned out. "Back in your car, mate. We can do this out of the cold." He thumbed the electronic key stuck on his dashboard and the gates swung open.

Mark looked torn, but Ciara came to the rescue. I hadn't realized she was there until she leaned out too and said, "Eva needs the loo. Right now."

If you don't know why that stopped all arguments in their tracks, you've obviously never spent much time with a three-year-old.

We followed Mark up the drive. He went straight to the main entrance and stopped the car. By the time we pulled up behind him, he was helping Ciara bundle the girls out of the back.

"Through the front doors, first right," Jay said to her, putting his code into the lock, and she scooped Eva up and ran.

Ruby, two years older and thoroughly scornful of toilet emergencies, launched herself at me instead, hugging my legs. "Hi, Uncle Luke. Am I still your favourite?"

"You're my favourite five-year-old," I told her. "Eva's my favourite three-year-old."

"When I was three I was your favourite, wasn't I?"

"And back then Eva was my favourite one-year-old." Time to change the subject. "Hey, Miss Five, why aren't you at school?"

"Because it's Saturday, silly." She beamed up at me, all big blue eyes, curly black pigtails, and mischief. "Daddy said *lots* of rude words about you in the car. Do you want to guess which ones?"

"I'll pass."

"I can tell you all of them, if you don't want to guess."

"Inside, Ruby-Roo," Mark said. He was still glaring at me, so I steered Ruby up the steps. If I was going to get yelled at, at least it could be out of the cold.

It was a shock to step back into the main foyer. I hadn't been in here for a couple of weeks, not when there were other entrances nearer the library. It felt echoey, a little too quiet, and I had misgivings at once. "We should go to—"

"Not until you talk to me," Mark said, stepping closer. "The *hell*, Luke? Is there no internet connection here? Did your phone break?"

"No."

"Then what the *fuck* is wrong with you?"

"Swear jar, Daddy."

Jay moved to stand at my shoulder, his shoulders tensing. "You want to back off a bit there, mate?"

"Okay," Ciara said, coming out of the loo. "Testosterone break, please. Little ears. Girls, go through those doors and see what you can find in that big hallway. Don't go anywhere else and don't touch anything that might break. Ruby, look after your sister."

"Don't touch the pictures or you'll set off an alarm!" I called after them as they ran off into the central hall. "Ciara, I don't think they should go off alone."

"Can they get outside? Get hurt?"

"No," I said uneasily. I was the only one the ghost had tried to injure, and she had yet to do anything but walk behind me during daylight. There had been nothing in any of the histories to suggest she had hated children, and generations of them had grown up here safely. "But—"

"They'll be fine." She came forward and hugged me hard. "Are you? We've been worried."

"I'm okay."

"Your mum rang me," Mark said. "She's frantic."

"I'll ring her," I said. "I'm sorry. I got caught up." I thought again. "Is everyone okay? Nobody's in trouble, are they? Dad's heart—"

"Only problem he has is worrying over you!"

Ciara said, "Darling, stop yelling. It's not helping." She looked back up at me, her pixie face suddenly stern. "You suddenly decide to move, tell everyone you want a fresh start, and then you go quiet for weeks. We thought...."

"I would *never* run," I said. "Guys, I'm so sorry. I didn't mean to scare you. It's been complicated."

"Yeah?" Mark said, drawing out the word as he eyed Jay over my shoulder.

Jay snorted. "Not that kind of complicated."

"Well," I said, "kind of that sort of complicated."

Ciara sighed and reached round me to offer Jay her hand. "Sorry. My guys suck at first impressions. I'm Ciara, nice to meet you. You are?"

"Jay." He shook her hand—and he must have smiled, because her eyes widened suddenly. "Charmed."

"Wow," she said and patted me on the cheek. "Okay, I forgive you. That's a good excuse right there, although mostly because I'm shallow and he's cute. Mark might take more work."

"Mark definitely will," the man himself said, although his tone was less aggressive.

I glanced up at Jay, who was looking a little flustered. "Okay. Guys, I love you, and I'm sorry, really I am, but you have the worst timing. We're in the middle of something here, and it's the bad kind of complicated. I don't want to get you involved."

Mark sighed, quick and impatient. "You're family, idiot, even if I'm pissed off with you. Of course we'll help. What's going on?"

"You're going to think I'm crazy."

"Nothing new, then," he said and grinned at me. "Spill."

"Well," I said. He probably wasn't far off shoving me in the back of the car and driving me to an intervention anyway.

"Place is haunted," Jay said, saving me the trouble. "Ghost doesn't like him much."

"Haunted?" Mark scoffed.

Ciara shivered, though. "It's definitely spooky. Luke, are you sure you're okay? If you're seeing ghosts—"

"Clanking chains, or apparitions floating around in sheets?" Mark wanted to know, his face bright with amusement. "Headless horseman? I've always wanted to see one of those."

"Don't joke!" Jay snapped out. "We just drove back from hospital. She tried to kill him. Twice."

In the silence that followed, a whisper came, sweet and slicing. *"Ten."*

Mark jumped, and Ciara glanced around, her eyes widening. "Who was that?"

"Our cue to leave," I said. "It's not even nine in the morning. Does she not sleep?"

"I'm thinking this is going to be an interesting explanation," Mark said, but his eyes were bright with fascination. "Girls! Time to go!"

There was no response, and I suddenly realized I couldn't hear their footsteps anymore.

"Ruby!" Mark shouted as Ciara called, "Eva! Come here!"

Still nothing.

"Nine," she said, her voice a little further away, down the corridor where the girls had been playing.

"Eva!" Ciara called again, her voice shaking. "Where are you, baby?"

"They can't have gone far," Mark said. "Right?"

"Short corridor," Jay said, starting towards it. "Gun room, commander's office, both locked, couple of pantries." He shot me a worried glance. "Stairs."

"Ruby knows better," Ciara asserted.

"Might not have heard us."

"I'm glad you know your way round," Ciara said, and I recognized the sound of someone talking to cover her fear.

"He works here," I said. "Keeps an eye on the place."

"Oh," Mark said with a note of interest. "Luke mentioned you."

"Eight."

"Ruby!" I called before anyone could react to that. "Eva!"

Still nothing, although we were in the stairwell now and the other rooms all opened out of here. Jay tried all the doors. All but one were locked, and that led into a small kitchen. The counters were still there, but a quick glance was enough to show us the girls weren't here.

"Upstairs?" Mark asked.

"Could be." Jay rubbed his brow, frowning. "Okay. No one goes anywhere alone."

"Seven."

"But," he said, raising his voice over her, "we take a floor each. Ciara, you and I check down here and then go back to the foyer."

"In case they come looking for us," she said. "Fine, but Mark stays with you."

"Why?" Mark asked.

"Upstairs is bedrooms, right? I'm small enough to crawl under beds."

He nodded and turned to Jay. "Lead on, Macduff. Let's find my girls."

"Six."

"Lay on," I corrected Mark, just to make him react. "Illiterate barbarian."

He didn't even lift a finger at me. Ciara laughed, though, a little shrilly, and followed me up the stairs. As I reached the first bend, Jay said, "Luke."

"Yeah."

"Be careful."

"And you," I said, trying to smile at him, and continued up the stairs.

As we got to the top, I heard, just ahead of us, *"Five."*

"Ruby!" Ciara called down the corridor. "Eva! Come out, come out, wherever you are! Please, girls!"

We checked every room, the lights sliding on as we walked. Most were locked, but a few of the big east-facing conference rooms were open. Ciara crawled under every table while I checked cupboards. Outside, the snow was getting heavier, falling in a slow, soft whirl that made the rest of the world seem very far away and deadened every sound.

"Four."

"Luke, talk to me," Ciara said. "I can't keep listening to that."

"Okay," I said, but words, which usually came so easily, seemed hard. "Think they're okay down there?"

She rose to her feet again, dust smudged across her cheek. "Hope so. Mark panics. It's why I wanted to come up here with you. I thought your Jay would keep him grounded."

"He's good at that."

"Three."

She shuddered. "Tell me about him. Tell me about anything. *Ruby*! *Eva*! Where are you?"

I gripped her shoulder. "Hold it together. You can do it. We'll find them."

"Talk about something else."

"Jay," I said as we ventured out into the corridor again, "Jay saves people. He's rescued me from her a few times."

"Two."

"He seems nice," she whispered, but she was glancing around nervously.

"He's...," I started and stumbled. I couldn't find one word to sum Jay up. "He's a good one."

"One," Ginevra sang, and with a soft stutter, all the lights went out.

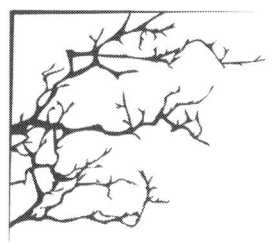

Chapter Fifteen

We'd left doors open behind us and a pale, wintry light still seeped into the hall, but it was too dark to see clearly. Faint shadows suddenly blurred into real darkness.

"Come and find us," Ginevra chanted triumphantly, and suddenly we could hear footsteps—not slow pacing this time, but running towards us along the hall, creaking quickly on the floor above, in the empty room we had just left, echoing and repeating in every direction.

And in the middle of it, suddenly and loudly, the sound of a child screaming.

It came from the library. I took off, Ciara at my heels.

We found Eva huddled into the empty shelves in the gallery, howling as tears ran down her reddened cheeks. As the door slammed behind us, she flinched and then, seeing us, launched herself at Ciara so hard she almost fell. Ciara grabbed her, crying herself, and Eva locked her hands in her mum's hair and clung, sobbing, "Mumma, Mumma."

"Ruby?" I called. "Come on, sweetheart. Game's over."

But there was no sign of Ruby.

Mark burst through the door below. "Eva!"

"We've got her," I called down and then frowned. "Where's Jay?"

"Right here," Jay said, coming in behind him at a slower pace.

"Have you found Ruby?" I asked.

He shook his head and beckoned us down.

Down on the main floor, the cold struck me. Snow was beginning to pile up against the windows, and the room seemed icy. The computer was off, and the desk lamp too.

"Power's gone," Jay said. "Heating too."

Behind us, Eva's sobs were subsiding to a steady hiccupping whimper. Ciara said, her voice fragile, "Baby, where's Ruby? Where's your sister?"

"Don't know." She pressed her face to Ciara's shoulder. "I don't want to play this game. I don't *like* it."

"What game?" Mark asked, rubbing her back. "What game were you and Ruby playing?"

"Hide-and-seek," she said. "The lady said we could."

"What lady?" I asked sharply.

"The one who lives here," she said, a little impatiently, and looked over my shoulder towards the shadows under the gallery. "That lady, Uncle Luke."

We all swung round, but there was no one standing there, not even the sound of breathing.

"She's gone again," Eva said matter-of-factly. "Mumma, I want to go home now."

"When we've found Ruby," Ciara promised.

"She's hiding."

"Where's she hiding?"

"I don't know," Eva said, her face turning cross. "It wasn't my turn."

"She's playing hide-and-seek with the ghost," I said. "She could be anywhere in this stupid fucking building, with that bitch trying to stop us from finding her, and I don't even know where to start looking, because everything I do know is just hypothesis, and—"

"Luke," Jay said. "Steady."

"We don't even know if she is Ginevra Treggio, or if she's still in the damn box, wherever it is, or whether the story has anything to do with—"

"We can check that," he said and turned to stride out of the library door. "Bring Eva."

Out in the north foyer, there was more light, although it was still dimmer than I'd ever seen it. Looking up, I saw snow had covered the cupola.

Jay went to the bottom of the stairs and pointed up at the picture. "Eva, was that the lady?"

She stayed quiet, a little uncertain of him, and Mark said, "Was it her, baby?"

"Yes."

In the dim light, Ginevra's smile didn't look quite so charming and mischievous. I could read malice into that painted face now.

"What's going on here?" Mark said. "Where's my girl?"

"I'll tell you as we look," I said. "Jay, back to Plan A. I reckon our best chance of finding Ruby is to find her."

"Attics," Jay said. "Need power."

"She's—"

"Blown a fuse, I reckon. Don't think she's up to power lines." He went back to the cupboard by the door. "Fuse box is here. Tell them about the ghost."

I did, hurriedly and maybe not that clearly. Mark looked ready to protest, but Ciara believed me. She tightened her arms around Eva and said, "What does she want with Ruby?"

"She wants to be found," I said and didn't voice my other fear. Four hundred years is a long time to play hide-and-seek by yourself. With the heating off, if we didn't find Ruby soon, Ginevra might have a new playmate.

The lights came on, and Jay stepped back with a grunt of satisfaction. "Had to replace six. Lifts should work now." He passed me and Mark torches and shoved one in his own pocket before picking up the crowbar we had used before.

"Attics," I said, remembering our earlier plan. "Basement. Stables. Exorcist."

"Attics. Basement. Phone call to base HQ. Royal Military Police, a hundred off-duty Micks, and a dog unit."

Mark looked a little taken aback, but I breathed in with relief. "God love the British Army."

"Damn right," Jay agreed. "Lifts. March."

We marched. There were no footsteps echoing us this time, just the soft patter of snow against the windows. We took the lift up in silence, except for Ciara whispering to Eva, who had cried herself into a half doze.

"Could wait with her in the car," Jay said, "or at mine. Ghost's only been there once."

"No," Ciara said with quiet certainty. "We stick together."

When we got up into the attics, they were dark. There were no automatic lights here, although there were skylights, gleaming grey. It was cold—so cold it hurt.

Jay swept his torch around, lighting every distant corner, and Mark called, "Ruby!"

"There's nothing here," I said, shivering hard. "It's empty. Why was she trying to get me up here if it's empty?"

"She's a bitch," Jay said. "Doesn't need a reason."

"It's cold," Ciara said, and that word went echoing out through the shadows. Ciara's voice was higher pitched than the ghost, but that word, in a woman's voice, made my shoulders tense. "It's so cold. You said you were almost hypothermic on the floor below. Is it this cold there?"

"No," I said. "Not quite." If I fallen asleep up here, I would have been in a much worse state by the time Jay found me. If he'd found me. Maybe it *was* company Ginevra wanted.

We walked the perimeter of the room, flashing torches under the eaves just to be sure, but Ruby wasn't there.

Back in the lift, Jay brought out a key that he used on the panel before hitting the lowest button. "Hard to get down here."

"Are there stairs?" Mark asked.

"Behind a locked door."

"If she can blow a fuse, I'm sure she can turn a lock," I said. "I don't think she can do much physical stuff, but small things, yes."

That, of course, was the moment when the lift suddenly jerked, the lights flickering out for a second before it reassumed its slow course downward.

"What was that?" Mark demanded.

"Backup generator taking over. Snow's probably brought a power line down somewhere," Jay said and got his phone out. The lift had come to a stop before he got through, but he just said, "McBride up at Eelmoor Hall. Need an assist."

As he explained, Mark and I stepped out of the lift. The lights came on as we moved, but only the one closest to us. We both gasped in dismay.

The attics had been empty, but the basements were full to bursting. Rows of wire-rack shelves were full of cardboard boxes. Crates, both full and empty, were stacked ceiling high. There was a nest of desks stacked over each other at dangerous angles and computer chairs piled up with their legs sticking out to cast bonelike shadows on the wall. To our left there was a row of bedsteads on end, and behind them, where the vaulted roof dipped down, were mattresses, some stacked and others leaning against them.

It was a maze, and that was just what we could see. Beyond, I could glimpse more vaults, more mess, fading into the dark.

"Ruby!" Mark shouted, cupping his hands around his mouth.

The name echoed away into the darkness.

Jay came forward. "Help's on its way. Snow's causing a lot of problems out there, but she promised to send extra generators as well."

"I can't just wait," Mark said, his voice cracking. "She's *five.*"

"We keep looking," Jay said. "Start at the bottom of the stairs. Circle outward."

He led us across the basement, twisting between piles of junk as the lights flickered on around us. Now, for the first time since we left the library, we all heard the echo of footsteps just behind ours.

The foot of the stairs was blocked off with a pile of whiteboard easels. None of us could have fitted through, but Mark shot forward, reaching out to unwind a long thread of curling black hair from one of the screws. "Kid sheds hair like a cat."

"So she was here," Ciara said. "But it's so cold. Why would she stay down here?"

"Easy to get lost," I said, looking around for a likely path. Where would Ruby have gone from here?

It was cold, and it felt like it was getting colder. My breath rose in a pale cloud in front of me, and I found my mind drifting to the snow, falling with a quiet menace.

"Luke!" Jay said sharply.

I shook myself. "What?"

"Spaced out there, mate," Mark said. He was rubbing his arms. "Can we please hurry?"

"Why's it so cold?" I asked, trying to get my head clear. "It wasn't when we got out of the lift."

"*Cold,*" a sad little whisper repeated, echoing out of some hidden corner. "*So cold in this box.*"

And, on the heels of the cold, the fear came rising up from the tiled floor. It didn't just sweep over me this time. I saw Jay's jaw tighten, Mark's face crumple, and Ciara's mouth fall open.

And Eva screamed, with the sort of pure terror that no toddler should ever have to experience.

Maybe that's what gave me the strength to fight back. Maybe it was just that, unlike the others, I'd faced this repeatedly, under worse circumstances than in a fully lit room with my friends beside me. Maybe it was because I wasn't bloody paralyzed for once. Whatever the reason, I found the strength to yell, "Stop it! Stop it, Ginevra! Leave us alone!"

I had her attention, could feel the weight of it, hear her breathing behind me.

"You didn't deserve this," I said to her as Ciara began to cry silently. "You deserved better. And so do we." I closed my eyes against the beating wave of her fear. "So did I."

The fear faded, but when I opened my eyes, I saw that the lights had gone too. For a moment, the only noise was Eva's tears, but then even she went quiet. Jay switched his torch on, lifting it to send a thin spear of light through the darkness.

And, very faintly, we heard the sound of banging.

"Ruby!" Mark yelled, and the banging got louder.

I moved first, probably just because I had dealt with the fear faster. Switching my torch on, I ran towards the noise, dodging between piles of dusty furniture, heaps of old folding desks, and metal lockers with their doors hanging open. There were cobwebs hanging from the ceiling in long trails, glinting in the torchlight, and a thick scent of damp cardboard, rust, and mouse.

The banging grew louder. The furniture was getting older with each step—a peeling beige sixties oven, mouldering armchairs with polka-dot prints, and, in the bob of light from my torch, an old freezer shoved against the wall, shaking a little with the force of blows from within.

I swerved towards it. At the same moment a voice rang out, a voice I knew at once, though it had been years since I'd heard it, loud and strong and urgent. *"Luke! Watch out!"*

It made me falter, bringing my torch round, and I saw the first sliding movement of the pile of tables and boxes beside me. It was enough of a warning for me to throw myself forward even as the pile toppled, collapsing down as if some unseen hand in the heart of it had reached out and simply pushed at the one spot that would unbalance the whole. I dropped my torch as I rolled across the floor, and it went spinning away—lighting up wall, ceiling, falling boxes, and Jay, ten steps behind me, lunging forward to pull Ciara and Eva away. Then the light was engulfed as a box split, spilling old saucepans in a clatter that drowned all other noises.

There was more, but the noise and loss of the torch left me unprepared for the first slab of damp cardboard slamming into me, knocking me down as it split. I was engulfed in old magazines, dust, and moths. I threw my hands over my head as more and more fell on me, burying me.

When the noise stopped, I clawed my way out, shoving aside unseen rubbish. My head was throbbing, and my shoulder hurt. My knee was bleeding in a thin hot line. I couldn't hear the others, couldn't see any torches. The only sounds were my own breath and its soft inevitable echo just ahead of me in the dark.

"Jay?" I called. "Mark? Ciara?"

No one answered.

I put my hand out, groping blindly for something that would tell me which way I was facing, where the floor was, what had happened.

And someone took my hand, pulling me back to my feet.

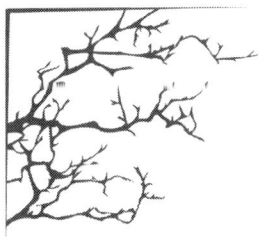

Chapter Sixteen

It wasn't Ginevra. This was a male hand, broad and strong. It wasn't Jay, either. I already knew his touch.

I knew this hand too, just like I'd known that voice calling my name.

I may have imagined it. I'd hit my head, and I was pretty disorientated. He didn't touch anyone else, and Mark, who was the only other one who would have recognized that voice, says he didn't hear it clearly. He assumed it was Jay calling me. Jay says it wasn't.

Even if I accept there was another spirit there, it could have been any of the other Eelmoor ghosts, coming forward to help me against one of their own. It could have been a heartbroken cavalier, finally home from the war.

But I believe, I *believe*, that Danny came back to me at that moment, when I needed him most.

A foot away, my torch clicked on. The hand in mine went cold and then insubstantial.

I picked the torch up and swung it round, orientating myself. She was still breathing in time with me, but I was no longer afraid. She had tried to kill me three times and failed.

Enough was enough.

Turning the torch back towards the heap of fallen boxes, I saw why I couldn't see other lights. The pile was so high that it almost reached the roof. It had crested up against the next heap of shelves, but there was still a small gap in the middle, at head-height on me. I shone my torch that way.

"Luke!"

Mark appeared in the space. He looked pale and shaky.

"I'm good," I said. "Are you?"

"Alive and in more or less one piece, all of us. Ciara's twisted her ankle, and Jay's—"

"Jay's fine," the man himself snapped.

"Jay's caught under the boxes," Mark said. "He's—"

"I'm *fine*. Get the kid."

I took him at his word and turned back to the freezer. It had been caught by the wave of boxes, knocking it away from the wall a little, and I had to move six or seven to get to the lid. Ruby was definitely in there. I could hear her hollering at the full extent of her lungs.

The lid was damn heavy, from an era before magnetic seals, and it took me two attempts to push it right back. On the second, Ruby came shooting up, pushing from below as I heaved from above. She continued all the way into my arms, knocking me back over, with a howl.

"I've got you," I told her, struggling to my feet. "Mark! Ciara! I've got her!"

"Daddy!" Ruby screamed, so close to my ear it hurt, and took off out of my arms like a greyhound.

Mark had just appeared around the far side of the pile, scrambling over the mess where it had fallen away from the wall. He dropped to his knees as Ruby hurtled towards him, holding his arms out to catch her. I staggered around them to climb out, torn between relief and worry for Jay.

He wasn't fine.

He was on the ground, his right leg curled up under him as he clutched at his left thigh. His left leg was trapped under the edge of an oak table that was trembling with every movement he made. I went to him, bracing my shoulder against it as well, and he looked up at me with sheer naked relief.

"Luke," he said, leaning in close enough to breathe against my cheek. "I heard it break."

I turned my torch onto the table edge again and saw where it had come down, just below the end of Jay's cut-off thigh. His jeans leg was flat beneath it. If there was anything left of his prosthesis, it must be in splinters.

"I can't get it off," he said, with such forced calm that I hurt for him. "And I can't get out until it's off."

"There's help on its way," I said, squeezing his hand. "Hell, if they're not here in ten, I'll go and hunt down a pair of scissors and cut you out."

"Have to be pretty sharp scissors," he said and then tensed. "Holy fuck."

"What's wrong?" I said, but he was staring past me.

Mark had just carried Ruby out from behind the pile, his torch bobbing awkwardly where he was trying to hold both it and an armful of shaking, sob-

bing little girl. Jay shone his light that way, his eyes widening. "I thought I saw....
There."

I turned to look. The beam was falling on an old wooden chest that was sitting against the wall. It must have been at the very back of the pile that had fallen on us, under decades, if not centuries, worth of junk.

"Does that look familiar to you?" Jay asked.

"It looks like the one in the library," I said. I swallowed hard. "Do you still have that crowbar?"

He nodded and passed it to me. "Get the kids away."

"Mark," I called without looking away from the chest, "get out of here."

"And leave you two—"

"Cavalry's on its way. They might need directions. And I don't want the girls to see what might be in that box."

He went, and Jay and I stayed there. Once the sound of their steps had faded, I stood up. As I walked to the chest, she was right behind me, breathing fast. I prized it away from the wall, inch by inch, leaving thick trails of dirt behind me, and then stepped around it to try to get it open.

I tried just lifting the lid first, but it wouldn't shift. I had to tuck the torch under my arm so I could wield the crowbar.

Have you ever actually tried to use a crowbar to lever something apart? It's harder than it looks. It took me three attempts to wedge the end into the crack between the chest and its lid, and it slipped out when I pressed down on it.

"Slowly," Jay said, but she was almost gasping behind me now, her breath catching in near sobs.

I tried again, and this time the lid rose with a slow groan. I crouched into it, putting all my strength into pushing it up, not even looking across until the lid suddenly crashed back.

Her breath caught. I swung the torch up to point into the chest.

And looked straight into her eyes.

I swear, for a moment, I saw her as she must have been: beautiful, vibrant, angry, her hair falling in tangles, her dark eyes blazing, her hands red with blood.

Then the illusion faded and I was staring at a dry and shrivelled thing, a mummified corpse in a white silk dress, her hands hardened into clenched fists.

I felt lips brush my cheek, cold and light as snow, in a single kiss of thanks.

And then Jay and I were alone in an echoing darkness that suddenly felt much bigger than it had before. I turned around and went back to him, reaching out to clasp his hands tightly.

He kissed me, on the other cheek, and said, "You were right. She did deserve better."

"I know."

"So did you."

"I know that too." But I thought of that warm hand in the darkness and let that old sorrow go, let Danny go. "It's okay now, though. I'm going to be fine without him."

"Good." He was quiet for a while before he said, "Luke?"

"Yeah?"

"Want to try someone who will stick around?"

"That would be nice," I said, trying to keep it light even as a tight, tense part of my heart suddenly relaxed. "Fair warning, though. I hold on to people pretty hard when I have the chance."

"Noticed that."

"And it's okay?"

He kissed me. "Don't scare easily."

"Good," I said and kissed him back.

THE CAVALRY TURNED up ten minutes later.

And by the cavalry I mean the Royal Military Police, of course, and a whole load of very efficient young chaps (And yes, Ciara, two chapesses too. Is this story a group collaboration now? No? Then stop reading over my shoulder and nit-picking.) with tools, energy, and the ability to efficiently extract Jay from the pile of debris, transfer us all to the ambulance or a nice sit-down with a hot cup of tea as appropriate, and only look mildly startled to be shown a centuries-old corpse in a wedding dress.

I lost track of some details after that, because when the army come in and take charge, they take charge. They whipped Jay off to hospital pretty quick. The same ambulance crew diagnosed Ruby with shock and me with mild concussion but decided neither of us needed to be taken in. She would be better off in the comfort of her own home, and I just needed someone to keep an eye on me.

I ended up in Mark's spare room and spent most of the afternoon on the phone, grovelling to Mum and Katie and then enduring a blistering call from the general who had hired me, who wanted to know what the hell I'd been doing looking for dead bodies in the basement instead of packing up books in the library. Ciara eventually took the phone away from me on that one, said some very ill-advised things about archaic neofascist institutions, and hung up.

"I think you just got me fired," I told her.

"You were nearly done with the job anyway," she told me and sat down beside me. "That was a day."

"I'm so sorry I dragged you all into this," I said.

She smacked my arm lightly. "Shut up. The ghost pulled you in. We just refused to let you go alone."

"It wasn't your fight."

Mark appeared in the doorway. "You're family. So, yeah, our fight too."

"But—"

He ignored me to crash on the sofa beside us. "They're both asleep with the light on. Eva's fine. Bit jealous of Ruby's plasters."

"What, aren't you?" Ciara said, leaning on him. "Damn, did you think to ask where they got them? Did you see them, Luke? They have rainbows on them."

Mark snickered. "Luke definitely needs some, then."

I had just enough energy left to raise a finger at him. I was suddenly feeling very jealous and more than a little lonely. They looked so comfortable there together.

But, unlike the last few years of watching them, I had somewhere to go and someone to see, a man who might turn to me and smile when I came into his room. Things were getting better.

AND THAT'S ALMOST THE end of the story.

I suppose I could tell you about the next few days—how Jay did smile when I walked in, and how thoroughly cranky he was for the next fortnight. His leg needed replacing entirely, though there was insurance to cover it. That meant a wait and new fittings, and relying on me to drive him around once he was out of hospital. The Army didn't fire me, but I hurried through the rest of the work at speed, very aware of the police tape that still fenced off a corner of the basement waiting for confirmation that the body was as old as we thought.

We got that confirmation and some fairly lurid press coverage, and a burial was arranged for the end of February.

I didn't attend the ceremony, although Ciara went. Other things were going on. Jay got his final release papers and started flat hunting, and Katie found me tenants for my flat. I decided commuting from Aldershot to London wasn't much worse than commuting across London, and that since we'd already lived in two rooms together successfully for most of a month, there was an obvious solution to both our housing woes. I found us some shared places to look round. (And got grumbled at for forgetting to tell him we were moving in together, and then forgiven, because... well, *he* says it was because I was right to claim it cost less that way. Liar.)

We ended up in a maisonette flat not far from the station in Farnborough, one with no steps to manage. I wasn't asked to unpack the archive after it moved, and I returned to my usual studies with relief.

And so it went on, and so I could go on. This is the rest of our lives. I could tell you that neither Eva or Ruby suffered any long term effects, although Ruby, now fifteen, loves telling her friends the story of how she once got kidnapped by a ghost. There are other things too which happened because of that winter (Jay, sitting above the sea in Genoa seven years later, turning to me to say, "Not going to kneel, love, but I am going to ask"), but they're not really part of this story. There's only one more important thing left, and it's the one that still makes me sleep a little uneasily.

IT WAS THE WEEK WE moved into the flat, the same week they finally buried Ginevra Treggio. We were in the throes of unpacking, both of us fighting the urge to give up and put our newly assembled bed to good use, when my phone rang.

It was Mark, and I could tell as soon as he spoke that he was crying.

"They found him," he choked out. "They found Danny."

"Alive?" I asked, though I was sure I knew the answer, had known it since that last morning in Eelmoor Hall.

"No," he said, and I could hear in his voice the same strange mixture of grief and relief that I was feeling.

I'm not going to repeat that conversation word for word. It was too painful, and I want to put this down as simply and cleanly as possible. Make of it what you will.

They found Danny's body whilst they were demolishing a row of derelict shops about a mile from the hospital he had taken me to. The shops had stood empty for years, even before the fire that had ripped through them about a week after Danny went missing, before the police search had got that far. He had been in the basement of the last one in the row, tucked in the bottom of the old coal chute. He'd been there for ten years. The investigators didn't know why he was in the chute, but if he had been sleeping rough in the basement, it might have seemed like a way to escape the fire. There were certainly enough traces left in his system to suggest he had probably been too high to understand exactly what was going on.

A workman had found him. They'd been about to start the demolition, he told the police, when he heard someone moving about in the basement. He'd gone to investigate, following the sound of footsteps, heard a tapping sound from the chute, and pulled up the hatch.

He never found the person he'd heard walking. He swore, though, that it hadn't been his imagination or the echo of his own steps. He'd heard her, he said—heard a woman sigh behind him as he reached for the hatch.

But there had been nobody there.

AND THAT, I SUPPOSE, is that.

You were right, Jay. It helped to write it down. I'm not sure it will get rid of the nightmares. Our brains aren't really that straightforward. It made me re-consider a few things, though. I don't like to think about Eelmoor Hall much, even though it's where we met. We've got so many other memories, good ones we made together. When I think of that winter, all I remember is fear.

But that's not the whole story. It's not even the most important story. I've noticed that, writing it all down, and it's made me wonder if I've been a little unfair to you, trying to pretend that part of our lives never happened. It wasn't just the month I got haunted, after all. It was the month I met you, and that's surely more important. You're far more important than some long-dead girl.

That's what I realized, writing this down.

This isn't a ghost story. This is a love story. It's the story of how I fell in love with you.

And it has a happy ending, like the best stories do.

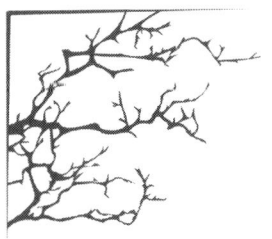

Author's Note

There's no such place as Eelmoor Hall, I'm afraid. That said, Luke and Jay's story draws on a great deal of local history and old English traditions. If you look very closely at a map of North Hampshire, for instance, in the little triangle of heathland between Aldershot, Farnborough, and Fleet you will find a place called Eelmoor Hill beside the Basingstoke Canal, although there is no mansion on its slopes. Eelmoor Hall was loosely inspired by the police training college at Bramshill House ten miles further to the northwest, and I have borrowed both parts of Bramshill's floor plan and one of its ghosts for this story. All other locations mentioned in the book are real.

There is no Royal Military School of Medicine. Aldershot does have a far more extensive museum dedicated to medicine in the armed forces, but it is in a modern and, as far as I know, unhaunted building in the Keogh Barracks, and nothing in this story is meant to represent it or any other aspect of real Army life beyond the integral and essential part the military play in local life.

As far as the historical detail goes, Sir Walter Tichborne was real and held the manor of Aldershot in the early seventeenth century, but his son Antony was my invention and their later family history is very different from the version presented here. The Battle of Alton took place as described, but as far as I know, there were no Tichbornes involved in it, although many members of the extended family fought in the Royalist armies.

The legend of the Mistletoe Bride was a popular one in the nineteenth century, and a number of stately homes in England lay claim to it, but it seems to be a popular invention with no basis in facts. Bramshill House claims to possess not only a replica of the chest she died in, but her ghost, who is supposed to wander the first floor and is particularly keen on the library in the Long Gallery.

Other Works by Amy Rae Durreson

About the Author

Amy Rae Durreson is a quiet Brit with a degree in early English literature, which she blames for her somewhat medieval approach to spelling, and at various times has been fluent in Latin, Old English, Ancient Greek, and Old Icelandic, though these days she mostly uses this knowledge to bore her students. Amy started her first novel a quarter of a century ago and has been scribbling away ever since. Despite these long years of experience, she has yet to master the arcane art of the semicolon. She was a winner in the 2017 Rainbow Awards. Twitter: @amy_raenbow

Read more at https://amyraenbow.wordpress.com/.

Printed in Great Britain
by Amazon

68527925R00085